DOCTOR BLAYDON'S DILEMMA

DOCTOR BLAYDON'S DILEMMA

Francis Hart

Chivers Press • G.K. Hall & Co.
Bath, England • Thorndike, Maine USA

This Large Print edition is published by Chivers Press, England, and by G.K. Hall & Co., USA.

Published in 2000 in the U.K. by arrangement with Robert Hale Ltd.

Published in 2000 in the U.S. by arrangement with Golden West Literary Agency.

U.K. Hardcover ISBN 0-7540-4012-7 (Chivers Large Print)
U.S. Softcover ISBN 0-7838-8863-5 (Nightingale Series Edition)

The text of this Large Print edition is unabridged.
Other aspects of the book may vary from the original edition.

Set in 16 pt. New Times Roman.

Printed in Great Britain on acid-free paper.

British Library Cataloguing in Publication Data available

Library of Congress Cataloging-in-Publication Data

Hart, Francis, 1916–
      Doctor Blaydon's dilemma / Francis Hart.
          p.   cm.
      ISBN 0–7838–8863–5 (lg. print : sc : alk. paper)
      1. Aged men—Fiction.   2. Surgeons—Fiction.
      3. Large type books.   I. Title: Dr. Blaydon's dilemma.
      II. Title.
      PS3566.A34 D63   2000
      813'.54—dc21
                                                              99–051867

CONTENTS

CHAPTER ONE

BACHELOR UNCLE

If one could remove the stars one by one, block the path of the rising moon, arrest time in space—or space in time, for perhaps they are the same—then nothing would move, nothing could grow older, nothing would ever change.

But there was no way to remove the stars nor block the moon nor arrest time in its processes, so everything did change and everyone, including Dr. Albert Branch, *did* grow older.

He said, 'I have performed surgical operations for forty years; before that, and along with it, I have also practised medicine. I have the skill in these hands to equal any feat ever done in medicine ... Have you any idea what rheumatoid arthritis means to me? Not the pain; I can get relief from that with one injection a day. I'll tell you what it means: I am old. God has let me age. And do you know what I think of that ? I'll tell you; I think man can become accustomed to anything—to one leg or one arm, to blindness or impotency, to paraplegia. Anything except age. He cannot ever properly adjust to age. My God! This is the most hopeless, senseless, useless thing—it takes away hope and spirit; a man is absolutely no good to himself or anyone else unless he has hope. *That's* what age does; it breaks you down into a cringing, hopeless lump of nothing!'

Dr. Branch drank off his second glass of scotch, blinked like an owl emerging from the dark, heaved up to his feet and said, 'Good night to you.'

No one spoke for a long time after he'd left the softly lit parlour of the huge old rambling house. It were as though all the honours that had been heaped upon Albert Branch, acknowledged by all as one of the finest surgeons of his day, lined the walls in their stiff frames, mocking.

The girl was young, perhaps eighteen or twenty but looking sixteen. She was extremely pretty; not just handsome nor attractive, she was entirely too much a perfect female for that. In fact an artist or writer might have seen fragile, blue-eyed beauty of a type rarely encountered anywhere. She wasn't very tall, perhaps five feet and three or four inches, but she had a lovely body, evenly proportioned, with no sags, no bulges, no lumps. Her lips were ripe and full, her nose not too thin, her hair a soft reddish brown, her ankles slim, her calves muscular. When she moved she seemed not just in motion, but in *symmetrical* motion.

Her name was Regina Barkley Branch. 'Queenie' her famous surgeon-uncle had

2

called her from childhood. It wasn't a name she liked especially; it was old-fashioned and awkwardly caressing in the way that a bachelor uncle might pat a little girl's head. But it had clung, like it or not. Dr. Branch was a man whose words, even pet names, had a way of being picked up by others.

The man sitting with her in the gloom of the great man's old-fashioned sitting-room moodily regarded a heavy seal ring on his left hand. He was as tall as the old doctor, his face had the same bony expression, the same deep-set hard, cold eyes, the same thin-lipped, critical mouth. But he was in fact no relation at all. His name was Andrew Connell. It had been O'Connell in his grandfather's time but there was no longer any point in commemorating an affiliation to the Auld Sod, so his father had simply dropped the O'.

Andrew Connell was a qualified doctor. He was in his early thirties but acted as if he were forty-five. When he spoke he was often broodingly sententious. When he moved he seemed to have no elasticity; seemed to be lost in thought more often than not. He would one day be a prominent physician. Not a surgeon; he'd already made up his mind he couldn't take any more schooling. 'Too much time has already slipped away,' he'd once told Dr. Branch. 'In any other profession a man's ready for the world at thirty. If I continued, and if I didn't do graduate work, or didn't tie myself to some hospital's damned apron strings for life, I'd still be bordering on middle age when I finally got round to taking off on my own. I don't want that; I never wanted that. I've got my profession, now I'll work at it as a general practitioner.'

It was Andrew who had made all the tests on Dr. Branch. 'Rheumatoid arthritis,' he said, pulling out each word from deep down as though he had to force himself to render that verdict.

That had been two years earlier.

Now he stopped staring at the ring, looked half defensively across at Regina and said, 'Liquor doesn't help at all.'

She nodded. 'He doesn't drink very much. Anyway, a gulp of water can't hurt a drowning man, can it, Andrew?'

'Your allegory isn't applicable.' Andrew got to his feet. 'In case you didn't recognise it, Regina, that wasn't the first drink he'd had this evening.'

The lovely girl flushed, looked away for a moment then rose. 'I'll see you to the door, Andrew.'

'I know where the door is,' he said a trifle rudely. 'Regina . . . ?'

'I'll watch him.'

'Give him coffee with his breakfast. You heard us discussing the operation he'll be doing tomorrow.'

She nodded, a little stiff-lipped, and

preceded him out into the hall to the front door. There, as he slouched past she said, 'Andrew—don't worry.'

He turned, on the verge of saying something sharp, then he simply nodded and departed. She closed the door, placed her back to it and squeezed her eyes so tightly closed that two tiny, perfect tears got caught in the thick, dark lashes. Then she took in a big breath and started for the staircase. She flicked off the sitting-room lamp as she passed by.

The house was old but sound, as most brick houses are that have been put together by unknown but wisely experienced hands. The banister up the stairs was as smooth as glass. No one could say how many people had used it, adding to that smoothness. Upstairs where the bedrooms lined a dim, rather lengthy corridor, there were two lights burning. One in an overhead globe mid-way down the landing, the other showing in a long crack from beneath the first closed door beyond the stairs. Her uncle was in there; he probably had some scotch in there too.

She hesitated briefly on the landing wondering whether she dared remonstrate, decided she didn't dare, and went along to her own room which was on the opposite side and half-way down.

She'd had that same room since early childhood. Its furnishings had changed as she had also changed. Now, the Mother Goose pictures were gone, the toys and games and ribbons were all gone. There was a white rug, thick and shaggy, a taffeta bedspread, an off-white full-length dressing-table and mirror. Two lovely occasional chairs and a desk. There were two racks of books and a reading-lamp beside one of the chairs.

It was obviously a girl's room, but there was something—perhaps the dark, solid bindings of the books—that made it seem as if a boy might also reside here. Her uncle had once jokingly told her she was more boy than girl in many ways. He'd said that although there were some learned men who doubted the merit of such people, he himself was perfectly satisfied that a few good old-fashioned male hormones made a woman a lot more worthwhile than no such hormones at all.

It was an odd observation to make to a young girl who, at that time, had been going through the torment and agony of becoming a young woman, but her uncle had always taken the long-term view of everything. Childhood, he'd held, was a swift phase, girlhood a prickly but temporary transition. As he'd said, 'You'll be a woman all your mature life, Queenie; concentrate on making the most of that, because when that phase passes—so will you.'

Her education had been less a source of learning than a definition of living. When she spoke of whatever intrigued her to her uncle, he'd take her for a walk and show her the wonders of nature. Or he'd explain what music did to a person—not just the hearing it, but what it did to them emotionally. He made life an adventure, living a challenge.

But he hadn't been very good at some things; the time she'd come to him heartbroken because a friend was moving out of the city, he hadn't known exactly how to fold her to his heart and kiss away the heartbreak. Instead, he'd asked Mrs. Moore, the housekeeper, to take her out to the confectioner's.

And the time, at thirteen, she'd discovered the boy she couldn't live without was seeing another girl at the same time, he'd taken her to a dress shop and let her pick out anything she fancied.

He wasn't a hard man, but he'd matured under a system that considered excessive emotionalism as something to be avoided at all costs. Yet he was sentimental; he had whiled away many a long summer evening telling her of his nephew—her father—and she'd seen the thin lips soften, the keen grey eyes turn milky. Not until she was much older had she discovered that he'd set aside a comfortable annuity to see his nephew through the university and medical school.

Her father had been his only living heir. When he and her mother died, Dr. Branch had taken a sabbatical; had gone off to America, North and South, and had come back full of wonderful tales. But some part of him had not returned with him.

She'd once in all innocence asked him why he'd never married. He'd gazed at her a moment, making her think he was displeased, then he'd smiled, taken her on to his knee and said, 'Queenie, if I'd been the one to write the old laws, I'd have allowed priests and ministers to take wives—but never physicians or surgeons. It's a poor life for a woman. Remunerative, yes, but a poor life.'

She hadn't fully understood that until about the time he sponsored Andrew and had spent a small fortune seeing him through the university and his medical training. She'd thought often since then that, although he might be right with respect to celibacy for doctors, he, of them all, should have been allowed one son.

And now he was nearing the end of the road that had been his life, his staff, his religion, his motivation, his purpose for living. She could understand much better than Andrew could— Andrew was just another man—what this was doing to him.

If he had another bottle of scotch in the lonely, austere bedroom with him, she prayed it might be in some small measure the kind of companion he should have had, and doubtless would have had, if he hadn't been such a harsh disciplinarian with himself.

She went to sleep thinking that and the

ensuing morning she still believed it.

CHAPTER TWO

BURLY HARRY

The memorial hospital was built upon the ground—once a cow pasture—where the earlier Queen Anne's Hospital had stood. It was modern and it was quite attractive. There were tall trees, a handsome greensward, cement walks winding among flowerbeds, and lots of large glass windows.

One's first impression of the Memorial Hospital was of a large library, or an elegant hotel. It did not actually resemble a hospital. It had a beautifully sculpted marble fountain in the centre of which water leapt and fell back forming aerated waves for the fat goldfish.

It was also, incidentally, the brainchild of old Dr. Albert Branch. He'd drawn up the plans and a delighted architect had translated them into wood and steel, into cement and stone, into pipe and glass and marble and tile.

But Dr. Branch's pragmatism had never once lost sight of the purpose of the Memorial Hospital. He had brought to it some of the finest medical teams to be found, he had badgered Boards of Directors, sympathetic laymen, national and international foundations. He had, in short, ensured the pyramiding wealth of Memorial at the same time he'd made absolutely certain that its staff and standards were of the highest.

He'd made enemies along the way, plenty of them, but a half century of any man's life and dedication are more than enough years to prove he is either right or wrong. Dr. Branch was right; eminently and indubitably so.

George Laxalt, Chief Administrator—a certified accountant among other accomplishments—once said that if one counted Dr. Branch's enemies, one could then multiply that number by ten and know the exact number of his supporters. Laxalt did not say his *friends*, he said his supporters, and that pleased old Dr. Branch, who believed far more in a heritage of intelligence among human beings ensuring their cold and practical rationality, than he believed in the kind of sticky emotionalism that made some men hero-worship other men.

As a surgeon the Old Man of Memorial had performed not only just about every operation known, he'd pioneered some that had kept other medical men in breathless expectancy. He'd had his failures, but his successes were far greater in number.

Andrew once said to Regina that truly great surgeons didn't appear in every generation as statesmen and soldiers did, but only once in perhaps every two or three hundred years. He

10

may have been right. Certainly the people of Memorial were convinced, even those who disliked the Old Man as an individual, that he was one of the greatest surgeons in a great many years.

It was inevitable, too, that Dr. Branch should have an ego. He was human, he was dedicated, he demanded perfection and achievement in others as well as in himself, and he would settle, likewise, for nothing less than success.

So, it appeared he'd been right about himself at least when he'd told Regina lifelong, dedicated surgeons shouldn't marry. Where would such a man, proud, irascible, impatient with dullards, a genius in his field, have ever found a woman who could have lived with such a temperament?

The day after he'd let his increasing despair show to Andrew and Regina—through the auspices of aged scotch—he'd performed a delicate brain operation, and afterwards, sitting exhausted in the private office of Dr. Blaydon who'd assisted, he'd said, 'Damn it, Harry, the pain was excruciating. It wasn't too hot in there; that perspiration was caused by other things.'

Dr. Blaydon was thirty-five years old, large, keen-eyed, assured, calm and quiet. He had come to Memorial from a surgical techniques professorship; among those who were qualified to know, which included Dr. Branch,

Harry Blaydon was one of the finest young surgeons in the nation. His speciality was neurosurgery.

Now he said, after lighting his pipe, 'You didn't deceive anyone, Doctor.'

Branch's bowed head came up, his hawkish old eyes probed. Dr. Blaydon put aside the spent match, heaved back in his chair and ran a hand through dark, curly hair. He was a handsome man in a very masculine way. His blue eyes contrasted strikingly with the black hair and brows. He returned the Old Man's stare, unperturbed.

'Everyone on the team understands tension, sir,' said Blaydon calmly. 'No one else was perspiring any more than was normal under those circumstances.' Blaydon puffed a moment. 'Liquor, incidentally, and as you damned well know, negates certain medications. If you're going to keep going, Doctor, you'd better do your drinking in the afternoon, not the evening, then, by the following morning, it will be out of your system and the injection to dull the arthritic pains will work. Otherwise it will not.'

Albert Branch, a man before whom many a renowned man had paled, sat and studied Blaydon's strong face for a long time before he said, 'Thank you for the prognosis, Doctor. I'll remember it.' He started to rise. Blaydon stopped him.

'Are we honest men, sir? If not, then of

course I have no right to be speaking to you in this manner. If we are, you won't be angry because I *did* speak to you like this.'

Blaydon rose, went over to the little hot-plate where he kept his private percolator working most of the day, drew off two cups of coffee and gave one to Dr. Branch, took the other one round to the desk and sat down again.

'You know; the hell of our profession is that while we make random achievements in many fields, we never seem to be able to discover what we want to know. How much research has turned up ways of healing this or that, or of arresting something totally irrelevant to what it was we were searching for? Arthritis is one of the oldest curses of mankind. The first or second human being to reach the susceptible age, probably had it. In the ensuing ten thousand years of spectacular progress we've found no prevention and no cure.' Blaydon looked up from his desk. 'What good is the art of heart-transplant, sir? We may be able to prolong a thousand lives a year in old, weary bodies. But arthritis, which is a million times more prevalent, baffles and defeats us. We find ways to do something spectacular for a thousand people, and can't keep one man's knuckles from ossifying!'

Dr. Branch drank his coffee, looked pithy, and said, 'I've always admired your brooding temperament, Harry. I've always felt that's

13

what it takes to be great in any field.'

Blaydon laughed. 'Brooding temperament? No, sir; disgusted would be a more appropriate definition. I don't care about a kidney transplant or a new heart in some old person. I want smaller achievements that won't ever get television coverage but will help men and women of twenty and thirty to lead productive lives for another fifty years. The hoop-la turns my stomach. I want progress, not filmed spectaculars.' Blaydon drank his coffee, pushed the cup away, took up his pipe and pointed it. 'Do you recall the Canadian who claimed to have corrected a paraplegic?'

'A damned fraud,' growled Branch.

Blaydon lit the pipe, smiling. 'Exactly. But he'd been a very renowned surgeon. The tragedy is that he succumbed to this craving for fame.'

'Well, of course our profession has its aberrants, Harry?'

'That's no answer, sir. What I'm saying is that generally, our dedication has been perverted to the hunger to be in the limelight. To the motivation of money. I say, sir, that the ego has no place in surgery.'

Dr. Branch finished his coffee. There was a faint reddish stain in his cheeks. He said, 'You are taking the long way round with me, aren't you, Harry?'

Blaydon nodded. He was not a very tactful man although in this instance at least he'd certainly tried to be. 'Whisky in the afternoon, sir, not at night. And what's in the future?'

'Five more good years, I should judge,' replied Dr. Branch, and finally rose. 'Thanks for the coffee; thanks also for the sermon.' The autocratic grey eyes, slightly yellowish now and faintly bloodshot, lingered on Blaydon's face. 'We have heart surgery in the morning. Good day.'

Harry Blaydon sat and smoked and minutely examined a black pen with sterling silver filigree that sat on an onyx base, the gift of a grateful patient who also happened to be a silversmith. He supposed that every hospital in the world, like every man who dominated it— and those who didn't think one man dominated each hospital didn't know much about the interior workings of hospitals— probably faced the same situation some day.

It was probably true, also, that most of those men recognised their own falterings in due time, and stepped down. But of course this could happen only where there was a little humility; if his ego drove a great man to cling to a throne, a premiership—or a hospital— then it was only it matter of time before something brought him down—bad planning, lethargic execution, a fatal and irreversible mistake.

The hell of it was, at Memorial, when this occurred, the next-in-command would be brought down too, because he'd tolerated

15

incompetence in the one field where people would not stand for it—in the daily handling of human lives.

In a way it was amusing. Kings and queens, presidents and dictators had been sending thousands to their deaths every year since time immemorial, and only historians were really morally concerned. But let one old man whose hands, arms, and joints were constantly inflamed and painful make one slip in an operating theatre, and that one life he lost became the substance of a murder.

Perhaps amusing wasn't the word; perhaps it was ironic, or sardonic, or even lethal, but to Harry Blaydon, who'd seen many people die on operating tables, life just wasn't all that important. The woodcutter in his forest admired each tree, but they were all just trees.

Well, one of the compensations of exclusive surgery was that when it was over someone else took over the patient; the surgeon had the rest of the day to himself. Dr. Blaydon had a habit that might have seemed strange to some; he liked to drive like mad as far out into the country as he could go, leave his car at a lay-by, climb someone's fence and go tramping over the valleys and hills. He loved nature; but it didn't have to be a stately oak or the cooling breeze of hilltops, nor even the summertime yields of endless panoramas beneath scoured skies. He even went tramping in the rain, in the sleet, in the wild winds. And he'd stop to

16

watch an old hog rooting for acorns, or a stolid cow chewing her cud.

None of this was actually so terribly odd; many a dweller in cement canyons renewed himself, or herself, in nature. What could have seemed strange was the host of acquaintances Dr. Blaydon had accumulated in this manner. There was an ancient horse he called 'Marengo', perhaps because it was such an appalling antithesis to Napoleon Bonaparte's beautiful Arab. And an old boar pig with a disagreeable temperament whom he'd named, 'Winston', possibly because, despite his slothfulness, the boar possessed depth and genuine perception.

And in a village called Leeswold he knew a dozen men, none of them very young, who gathered at a place named The Gargoyle to tell fantastic stories, drink beer, exchange morsels of local gossip, drink beer, and in their sly-raffish Anglo Saxon way, measure every stranger for the amount of beer he might be prevailed upon to stand the house, meaning of course, the men who hung about there.

At The Gargoyle Harry Blaydon was viewed as a burly, likeable chap who never spoke of himself but who sat and listened, and laughed, and looked successful enough. They'd long ago come to the conclusion he was some kind of city merchant who perhaps had been country bred and hied himself back whenever he could. They didn't really concern

17

themselves too much; he bought the beer and was a good companion. He might come in dripping with rain or stained with mud. They were in unanimous accord that he was a stout fellow; some of them hadn't even heard his last name and referred to him only as 'Burly Harry'.

That's where he went the day of his talk with Dr. Branch; out to Leeswold to The Gargoyle. But he laughed less and smiled with a distant shadow across his face.

It didn't matter; he stood the rounds and was a top-notch chap, was Burly Harry.

It was summertime, then, with high-sailing clouds, with a warm sun showing—when it wasn't raining—and in rural Leeswold the hangers-on were thinned down a bit by their field-labours. It was the best of all times to drink two or three pints, Harry's purse permitting.

The fields were green, the trees in full leaf, the streams alive with timid minnows and all across the rolling land were the troops of cloud-shadows charging and countercharging, mingling and always moving, carrying on the endless war of Nature in absolute silence.

To those living out their lives around Leeswold, or for that matter any rural village, everything natural was taken for granted. To Harry Blaydon who had, in fact, been reared in cities, it was all something of a private covenant that required renewing and which never, ever, remained the same.

CHAPTER THREE

AUTUMN

Transferees, or outright referrals made up a large proportion of Memorial's surgical-ward patients on the fourth floor. Once, a collision at sea had filled the place with burned and broken seamen, another time an epidemic-like siege of tumours had taxed all resources. But since those days enlargement of patient-facilities had made any such recurrence highly unlikely.

About the time Harry Blaydon became part of the staff, two terribly distinguished men had arrived, one from the Near-East, one from the Continent. They had been repaired and discharged without fanfare. After that one could expect at least one renowned individual to be in one of the private rooms on the fourth floor almost any day. This was of course good for Memorial's international image, local prestige, and treasury.

It also ensured that any doctors with ambition—and enough brass—would apply for a position on the staff. The requirements being very stiff, only the most competent ever made it, and as for people like Andrew

Connell who had actually no specialisation, the way in was barred. General practitioners belonged elsewhere, notably in villages or suburbs, or in private practice in towns or cities. At best they were viewed by some of Memorial's genuinely knowledgeable specialists, as witch-doctors; they never cured anything, they simply diagnosed ailments, then told the patient how to help his system overcome the illness. Usually the prescription amounted to dosage with aspirin, plenty of rest, warm food, no draughts and no worry.

Nothing really wrong with that, of course, except that no one really needed a medical degree to dispense such advice, and in the case of the very healthy, they would invariably recover in due course without the G.P's help. It was this rationalisation that got G.P.s viewed as witch-doctors, or at the very least, tolerable do-gooders around Memorial.

Andrew, perfectly aware of the distinction, visited Harry Blaydon in the autumn with a private feeling of inferiority, and because Andrew's temperament was susceptible to hot flashes, he was almost rude as he and Harry sat talking in Dr. Blaydon's small office. He said, 'If you wish to destroy him, Doctor, or perhaps to succeed him here as Director, all you have to do is allow this travesty to continue. I can tell you from experience that no man of seventy can continually use drugs and liquor without some kind of personal

20

disaster ensuing.'

Harry bit down on his pipe-stem. He'd met Andrew before. Also, Harry was a fair judge of people. He leaned towards Andrew and said earnestly, 'I don't much like your suggestion that I might be deliberately contributing, Andrew.'

'What else can it be, Doctor? Directly or indirectly, you're helping it to happen.'

'Andrew,' said Harry Blaydon quietly, 'I do not run the hospital. I cannot appear before the Board of Governors and say, 'That old man is going to kill someone one of these days unless you boot him out'.'

Andrew smiled. 'I can, Doctor. I have no private axe to grind. I've known Dr. Branch all my adult life. I think even his niece, whom he also brought up and educated, could be persuaded to tell the Board how much he drinks in the afternoons; how he's coming apart all over.'

Harry leaned back in his chair. 'His niece ...?'

'You've met her, Doctor; Regina Barkley Branch.'

'Well, yes, I've met her, but it was some years back. She was a child. As for getting her to appear against him ...' Harry looked quizzical. 'Would she actually do that?'

Andrew's bony face darkened, his lips lifted in a hint of a sneer. 'The variety of loyalty you're implying, Dr. Blaydon, died with Kipling and Walt Whitman.' The sneer

21

vanished, Andrew leaned forward. 'No one has the right to permit murder out of loyalty. No one at all!'

Harry almost smiled. 'Very noble,' he murmured, disliking Andrew more than ever, and he'd never actually felt drawn to him despite the fact that Dr. Branch invariably praised the young man. 'Very noble, Andrew, but you're overlooking the natural safeguards—surgeons are subject to annual examining boards.'

'Once a year,' said Andrew. 'After that they are free to perform operations for another twelve months. It may be hypothetical, Dr. Blaydon, but let me ask you this: What happens if in that twelve-month period the surgeon drinks heavily, and deteriorates so fast—because he is already diseased and old— that he commits a murder? Inadvertent murder, Doctor, but still murder. What happens?'

Harry's answer was short. 'Prove it, Andrew.' Harry rose, looking at his watch. 'You'll have to excuse me.' He walked out of the office angry and upset.

It wasn't what Andrew Connell had implied, particularly, that annoyed him, it was that he himself was caught in the middle of a very nasty dilemma.

He hadn't any operation to undertake that day; he'd only given that impression to get rid of Andrew Connell. Down in the first-floor restaurant—Memorial also had its own chemist's shop, barber's shop, florist's and outpatient nursing agency—he sat alone eating a sandwich and wondering if Connell hadn't something more by way of personal motivation than just his supposed altruistic viewpoint.

'Harry . . .'

He looked up. It was Dr. Branch in a floppy white coat. He said, 'Please do, sir,' and nodded to a loitering waitress who came directly over for the Old Man's order. Everyone at Memorial deferred to him, even the people on the mezzanine. Branch said, 'Lettuce and tomato salad, please,' then looked across at Harry Blaydon. 'What is it tomorrow? I forget. Sometimes they seem to run together.' He smiled. 'I'm getting old, Harry.'

'Spinal,' said Harry, finishing his sandwich. 'How's Regina?'

Dr. Branch's tufted brows shot up. 'Regina? Why, she's fine. Why do you ask?'

'Do I need a reason, sir?'

Branch thought a moment. 'No; but you haven't often enquired about her.' The piercing grey eyes suddenly narrowed. 'Or have you seen her lately?'

'No. But she must be a big girl now.'

'Twenty. It's impossible. How could little Queenie be twenty years old. Why, only last summer we went down to Summerfield and rented a cottage on the beach and I taught her

23

to swim.'

Harry gently smiled. 'That was a hundred, maybe even two hundred, spinals, cranials, neuros, ago, sir, not just one summer or one year. How are the hands?'

Dr. Branch swiftly and unconsciously shot a look at them. 'Fine, just fine. How've they behaved lately?'

'Perfect,' said Harry.

Branch's eyes remained unwaveringly upon the younger, heavier man as he said in a joking tone, 'Then you won't appear against my renewal before the Board.'

Harry matched the smile and shook his head, but he couldn't quite force himself to say aloud that he would not.

Fortunately Dr. Branch's salad came at that moment so Harry's silence was lost in the diversion. A moment later Harry asked how Andrew was, and Dr. Branch, fork poised, gave his head a little annoyed shake. 'From an adopted son he's become a gadfly, a guardian, a skinny bully.'

'And Regina?'

'Oh, no, Queenie doesn't change.' Suddenly Dr. Branch lowered his fork and stared hard. 'What are you probing for, Harry? Why all the questions?'

'Interest, sir, just personal interest. I apologise if it seemed like snooping. Friends have the right, I've always thought, to be interested. It's different from curiosity.'

24

Dr. Branch weighed all that, then resumed eating. Harry switched the subject, began discussing the forthcoming operation and soon had the Old Man talking volubly. People responded to whatever vitally interested them, even great and renowned people—or perhaps they were more susceptible than lesser people. In any case by the time Harry and Dr. Branch were ready to depart Regina and Andrew had been totally forgotten.

George Laxalt met the Chief Consultant and Assistant Chief just outside the lift on the fourth floor. He greeted them both then said, 'Received a call a few minutes ago about some African president flying in tomorrow for an examination.' Laxalt smiled. 'VIP—very important personage.'

Dr. Branch didn't smile. 'There's been an examination of course,' he said.

Laxalt nodded. 'Brain tumour suspected. That's all they'd say over the telephone but his personal man is coming along.'

Branch nodded. 'Make the arrangements, George. Private room, fourth floor, private nurses, all that.' He looked at Dr. Blaydon. 'What did you have planned for tomorrow afternoon, Harry?'

Blaydon smiled easily. 'I'd planned on examining an African president for a possible tumour, sir.'

The ghost of a smile touched the Old Man's thin lips.

Exactly,' he said, and walked off leaving Laxalt and Harry standing together outside the lift.

Laxalt shook his head. 'Most remarkable *old* man I've ever seen.'

Somewhere inside Dr. Blaydon a switch clicked closed. He looked at his watch, looked at Laxalt, then said, I'll be gone the rest of the afternoon. Post that information, will you please, George?' then he walked towards his office without awaiting confirmation.

There was a gong-system on the fourth floor to keep everyone apprised of the correct time. It sent softly melodious, chiming sounds up and down the corridors at the hour. As Harry Blaydon was getting into street clothes the gong signalled a very musical two o'clock in the afternoon.

He left the hospital at two-fifteen and was well on his way into the residential section of the West End by two-thirty. He looked full of honest resolve until the moment he slowed at the kerb outside the handsome old brick house of Dr. Albert Branch. Then he didn't look quite so determined.

Still, he persevered.

When Regina opened the door they stood looking at one another. Regina finally smiled but Harry Blaydon seemed to doubt himself. He finally said, 'Regina Branch?'

She laughed. 'You need glasses, Dr. Blaydon. A couple of years couldn't make all that difference.'

But they had, the Lord knew; they'd made such a difference. Harry stepped in, removing his hat and still having difficulty in concealing his astonishment. It wasn't just the short, sophisticated hair-do nor the modish dress that left no doubts of Regina's total womanhood, it was the calm, wise expression of the face and the gently chiding look in the beautifully soft eyes.

'Well, I think it's been slightly more than three years, not two,' he said, taking the chair she'd indicated. 'And as I think back, you seemed—young—for your age in those days.'

'Immature, Doctor? Didn't you mean immature instead of young?'

She was laughing at him. She also seemed to blossom under his admiration. He shrugged. He'd come here to ask some grave questions and get some grave answers. It hadn't occurred to him at all that this kind of sidetracking might ensue; he wasn't altogether prepared to cope with it, either.

She stopped smiling. 'Is something wrong at Memorial, Dr. Blaydon?'

'Memorial is fine,' he said. 'There's nothing wrong—precisely.'

'Precisely?' She picked that word up at once and leaned a little forward to study him more closely.

He looked round the room; it was massively furnished, seemed gloomy, seemed frowning

27

down at him from every corner. He rose, still holding his hat. 'I wonder if you'd do me a favour, Regina?'

'Why certainly, Dr. Blaydon; if I can.'

'Come for a little drive with me in the country.'

Her brows arched slightly. 'A drive into the country . . . ?'

'Yes. You see I'd like to talk with you and it just seems out of place here.'

Comprehension seemed to shadow her steady eyes. 'Yes,' she murmured quietly. 'I think I understand. Of course, Dr. Blaydon. Just a moment while I get a coat.'

After she'd left the room he went to a window, saw ripples of wind lifting and tossing leaves and odd bits of paper, saw the bare limbs of scourged trees, saw the grey-scudding pre-winter sky, and grimaced. The day matched his mood.

She returned with a little knitted hat framing her face and a matching scarf tucked neatly at the throat of her coat. They exchanged another solemn look, then he held the door for her.

CHAPTER FOUR

FACE TO FACE WITH FACTS

Man being largely a creature of habit, when preoccupied he may ordinarily be expected to act or react in some predictable manner although, as in Harry Blaydon's case, it wasn't entirely in his own best interests. He pointed his car in the direction of Leeswold almost without thinking.

It didn't occur to him then, nor even after he'd spied the village ahead and was within its limits, that taking young and beautiful Regina Branch there, where he was known, would be viewed with candid and fruitful interest.

They hadn't said very much on the drive except when he pointed out something in the scenery or commented upon the exhilaration of windy autumnal days in the country.

Her replies were polite, restrained, very proper. Once or twice she studied his profile but whatever was in her mind she kept there.

It was mid-afternoon when they stopped outside the inn at Leeswold. As he helped her to alight he saw the four idlers out in front of The Gargoyle turn to stone, their eyes sprung wide open. He waved. They nodded back. At Regina's look of interest he said, smiling, 'Friends. I stand a few rounds down there now

29

and again.'

She was interested. Holding her coat close against the chilly wind she looked around at the old chimneys, at the brickfronts, at the worn pavement and kerbs.

'Is this your village, Doctor?'

'No, not really. I just like to come down here once in a while. Come inside; we'll have some tea and talk.'

When she removed her hat, inside the inn, the greatest single benefit to wearing short hair became immediately apparent; it clung to her head like a halo of dark copper, not a hair out of place.

They ordered. She had only tea but he, who'd missed lunch or breakfast, one or the other since the only meal he'd thus far consumed had been before twelve with Dr. Branch, had roast beef. She smiled at him. 'Do you always eat like that? You'll get fat, Doctor, and you know what cholesterol does.'

He smiled, fumbled for his pipe, got it going, and said, 'You've guessed, of course, why I came to see you!'

'I think so.'

'That makes it easier!'

'Does it?' Her blue eyes were as steady as stone. He fidgeted on his chair. 'What's to be done, Regina? I hate my role as Judas, but it can't continue. Andrew Connell came round to see me. He implied that you knew just as much as he knows!'

Her face darkened slightly. 'What right has Andrew to do a thing like that?'

He gently shook his head at her. 'Regina, we're adults. I didn't like it any better than you like it now, but Andrew's not entirely wrong. The question isn't a matter of Andrew anyway. It's a question of your uncle. I want—I *need*—your help.'

'In what way, Doctor?' she asked softly. If he'd known her better he'd have been warned by that subtle softness.

'Persuade him to give up.'

'Leave Memorial?' She said it as though Harry had made an improper proposal.

'Cease to be a practising surgeon, Regina. Become a surgical adviser, an emeritus at a teaching hospital. The pay is a little less but that can't mean much to him. The prestige, if anything, would be more. He'd be in demand worldwide.'

She allowed the waitress to serve them and avoided Harry's face until the woman had silently departed. Then she sweetened her tea, sipped it, put the cup down and said, 'I couldn't persuade him any more than you could. By now you certainly know him as well as I do. Anyway, Dr. Blaydon, I wouldn't hurt him if my life were at stake. I just couldn't do that.'

Blaydon stopped eating to gaze at the lovely woman. She still seemed a girl to him. He had to remind himself over again that she was not.

31

It would be interesting, he thought, to look into her heritage and diet; she had an absolutely flawless complexion. It was the colour of new cream. She was really quite exquisite.

'Are you staring, Doctor, because you can't understand how someone could refuse to hurt another person?'

He shook his head, ate a moment, then said, 'Promise me you'll say nothing of this visit to your uncle; that you won't let him find out Andrew came to see me.'

'I'll promise that, yes. You're in a difficult position, Doctor, and I can appreciate it.'

'No, you can't. Not really, Regina. If he makes a serious blunder it'll bring me down right along with him. But more than that—someone has threatened to appear against him at the annual Board of Renewal examination.'

'Who?'

'It doesn't matter. What does matter is that he's caught up in a hopeless cycle. Scotch, arthritis, pain-killers. A *young* man couldn't keep it up indefinitely. For an old man it's courting disaster. The hell of it is, when the disaster strikes, it may be some distinguished man lying anaesthetised under his hands in the operating theatre. For example, what finally gave me the courage to come to see you was the report that some noted African will arrive at Memorial tomorrow with a possible brain tumour. Hypothetically, let's assume your uncle's hands malfunction on this man.'

'They wouldn't.'

'They could, Regina. That's my point. *They very well could.* I'm not afraid for myself; wouldn't it be much better for him to stop now, than to keep on until some disaster *does* arrive?'

She finished her tea, shook her head when the hovering waitress swooped down, then settled slightly in her seat and soberly watched him finish his meal, finish his tea, and pick up his cold pipe.

'It could happen, couldn't it?' she whispered.

'Yes. And I need your help very badly to prevent it from happening.' He was encouraged by her sad look. He was also touched by it. He reached over to pat her hand. 'We won't look very noble in our own eyes, I'm afraid, but it'll be quite enough to know that what we're trying to accomplish is absolutely right.'

'Andrew,' she murmured. 'He's the one who has threatened to appear before the Board, isn't he?'

He withdrew his hand. 'Forget Andrew.' It suddenly dawned an him there might be something personal between those two. He immediately corrected himself. 'Well, at least let's leave Andrew out of it for the present. What I need is for you to help me devise some way to save your uncle from himself.'

'How, Dr. Blaydon?'

He didn't know. 'Shall we discuss it on the drive back?'

When they emerged from the hotel dining-room the men out in front of The Gargoyle were conspicuously absent. Dr. Blaydon didn't notice that; didn't in fact even think of those men as he closed the door on Regina, slid under the wheel and started the drive back.

She said, 'Andrew's been after him not to drink so much in the afternoons.'

Harry's somewhat sardonic comment on that score was: 'Better in the afternoon than at night.'

Regina seemed not to have heard. 'I just don't see what can be done.'

Dr. Blaydon saw; he'd thought about it on their drive to Leeswold. But he was too discreet to mention it just then. Instead he told her, again, that although he was always at her uncle's elbow in the operating theatre, when the inevitable mistake came it would prove fatal to someone. But that wasn't altogether what motivated him; he just wasn't privately so much imbued with the idea of the sacredness of one human life. It was the Old Man he was thinking of; if disaster arrived Dr. Albert Branch wouldn't be the first renowned man who'd permitted his stubborn ego to carry him to the brink—then over it to disgrace, shame, and calumny.

He said, still working on what he thought

34

would be her female compassion, 'Having a conscience can be a detriment to a surgeon, especially if it's a lively one. Most surgeons, after enough people have passed under their knives, become somewhat hardened to the facts of life and death. But I've never yet met one who didn't dread the thought of bunglingly killing someone.'

She looked at him. 'Then why doesn't Uncle Albert stop of his own accord?'

He didn't answer that one; it was loaded and he knew it. He countered with a question of his own. '*You* tell *me*, Regina.' Then he looked at her and smiled. 'No, it isn't necessary. Everyone is entitled to their pride.'

'Unless it endangers others. Is that it, Dr. Blaydon?'

'Isn't it?' he countered, and watched her turn to gaze out of the window at the raw, wind-cowed countryside which was as grey and cheerless as autumn countrysides often are.

'What will he do—afterwards?' she eventually asked.

'Become what he's really most eminently qualified for, Regina. Surgeons of his eminence in an advisory capacity are very rare. It's no dishonour at all. Everyone, some day, reaches an age when their superlative knowledge, providing they've been as eminent in their field as he's been, is worth much more in an advisory capacity than it is worth in the operating theatre.'

'Doesn't he know that, now?'

'He knows it, of course, but it's rather like asking a mother to stop loving her one child and start supervising a lot of other children. He's been a surgeon for nearly half a century; a good many of the techniques used round the world were his innovations. I used to teach them myself. Surgery—medicine—is his life.'

'You have no idea how true that really is,' she said, looking at him. 'He once told me if he'd been making the laws he'd have prohibited surgeons from marrying.

Harry looked slightly shocked at that. Then he smiled, and finally he laughed. It was an infectious, booming kind of laugh. She smiled, wanly perhaps, but at least she smiled.

'There might be a lot fewer surgeons then,' he said, looking over at her, amused.

They arrived back before the big brick house as the sullen sun began its grudging descent, red and dull-looking. He saw her to the door, held her hand a moment and said, 'I'll ring you in a day or two.' He smiled down into her face. 'I'm glad you will help, Regina. I'm also very glad we talked.' He squeezed her fingers, turned and went back to the car.

On the drive back to Memorial he recapitulated all that had happened. It had come about just as he'd thought it might except for one thing; he most certainly hadn't expected her to be as he'd found her—a woman such as one usually only encountered

36

in paintings. Lucky Andrew—the insufferable puppy.

There were calls waiting when he got back. One was from George Laxalt, the other was from a member of the surgical team Dr. Branch had posted for the following day. He got Laxalt on the telephone first.

'Blaydon here.'

Laxalt sounded relieved. 'Glad you're back, Harry. The physician accompanying the African politician was on the wireless shortly after you left giving his report on the diagnosis made in Kenya or Zambia. Dr. Branch spoke to him, then asked me to inform you that it sounded to him like a massive malignancy.'

'That,' said Harry, 'is that. We'll confirm when the patient arrives. I'll speak to Dr. Branch before he leaves this evening.'

'He left an hour ago.'

Harry blinked. 'Left?' He couldn't have gone home or Harry would have encountered him when he'd returned with Regina. That thought chilled him through and through, too. He never could have faked some excuse old Branch wouldn't have seen through.

'Went shopping, I believe. Anyway, you'll have to catch him first thing in the morning.'

Harry agreed, rang off, lit his pipe and blew out a big sigh. Close call, that.

He then called the surgeon who'd wanted to contact him. That conversation was crisp and to the point. The other man, Norman Belden,

37

was fiftyish, grey, thin as a rail and utterly humourless. But he was a very good surgeon. In his brusque, toneless voice he said, 'Harry— Dr. Branch says this incoming patient from Africa may be terminal. I suggested that if tests confirm this we do not operate at all. Better for the man to die in bed. Better for international relations; better for Memorial too. What are your views?'

Harry was careful here. Dr. Belden was an ambitious, relentlessly efficient man, like an automaton. 'I'll discuss it with you in the morning,' he said. 'Let's get the tests completed first.'

He rang off, sat at his desk a moment puffing up clouds of smoke, then he rose, said 'Damnation,' and walked out into the quiet corridor ready for the trip home and eight hours' sleep, which he badly needed. It had been a day of bumps and grinds and harrowing close calls.

CHAPTER FIVE

A TEMPORARY REPRIEVE

The African arrived. He was an old man. somewhat more grey than black; his eyes were small, close-set, and yellowish where they should have been white, which of course was the Memorial medical team's first indication of his physical condition. Dr. Branch himself escorted the patient to the laboratory where tests would be made.

Harry Blaydon and Norman Belden went down to the restaurant for a cup of coffee and some talk. Belden's thin, long, grave face showed by its expression what he thought.

'The man will never recover from an op. in his present condition, Harry. If my guess about the tests is confirmed, he won't come through even if we keep him here a month or two building up his strength for the operation.'

Harry clung to his earlier position. 'Let's wait and see what comes of the tests.'

Belden raised cold, keen eyes. 'Of course.' He drank coffee, tapped the table as he glanced round the nearly empty large room, then he stopped tapping, leaned forward and said, 'Harry, there's another consideration.'

Dr. Blaydon remained silent. He had a premonition. Although he and Dr. Belden had never discussed it before, Harry was uneasily sure he knew what was coming. After all, Norman Belden was a very good surgeon; he would recognise any deviation from sound practice in another surgeon. Harry glanced at his watch as though to imply discreetly that he had to be elsewhere. That didn't deter thin, intense Dr. Belden.

'Branch can't do this one, Harry.'

Blaydon quietly sighed and raised his eyes.

The premonition had been correct. Belden went on.

'You're not blind. You know exactly what I mean, Harry. I'm surprised ... I've been waiting all the year for you to take the first step. Why haven't you?'

Being between two grindstones was not exactly a new sensation for Harry Blaydon; he'd learned long ago to live with tension. But this was different; this was like living inside a pressure-cooker.

Belden sat there waiting for his answer. He was a dedicated, dry and forthright man. He'd accept no evasive nor platitudinous answer. Harry spoke slowly.

'As far as the African is concerned, Norman, you've probably answered your own question. There may be no point in surgery. That's why I've said we ought to wait and see.'

Belden's thin shoulders hunched forward, his narrow face grew wire-tight. 'And after this African, who is next? It doesn't make any difference whether it's some international figure or not, Harry, the Old Man can no longer be relied upon. Don't tell me you haven't noticed the swelling in the joints of his hands. You couldn't have avoided smelling liquor on his breath; after all, you're closer to him than I am.'

It was a clear accusation. Harry accepted it as such; it simply verified what he'd told Regina: When Dr. Branch fell, he would drag

Dr. Blaydon down with him. No man could sit there with the spectre of his life's work being irretrievably smashed before his very eyes and not feel a little ill.

Harry glanced again at his watch. 'Let's go up and check on the tests,' he said, preparing to rise. 'And Norman—I have no intention of seeing Dr. Branch destroy himself, or you—or me—or bring disrepute upon Memorial.'

Belden had to be satisfied with that. He hadn't wrung any shamefaced admissions from Harry Blaydon, and that may have been a disappointment to him because he was a relentless perfectionist, but when he rose to cross to the lift he seemed less tense and hostile than he'd been at the table.

When they arrived back on the fourth floor a deferential registrar informed Dr. Blaydon that the African's personal physician, a man named Geoffrey Saul, was in Dr. Blaydon's office waiting to see him. Harry would have preferred having a private interview but Norman Belden went resolutely along with him.

Geoffrey Saul was a small, wiry, tanned man in his early or middle forties. He explained that he was a general practitioner, that he'd been the old African's personal doctor for the past two years, and although he'd often warned his patient he really should have competent and thorough physical examination, the old man had always put him off, saying

41

conditions in his country were too critical.

'So now,' said Saul, with a little shrug. 'There are the preliminary reports!' He pointed to Harry's desk.

Norman Belden made a typical remark. 'Anyone with your training should know the dangers of this kind of delay.'

Saul gazed at Norman for a moment as though to ask what, exactly, Norman would have done in Saul's position. Then he turned his back and watched Harry come round the desk and study the reports. He said nothing.

For Harry it was almost a relief to discover that the old African's link with life was well beyond the point of no return. He passed the reports to Norman and asked Geoffrey Saul to be seated. He offered him tobacco but Saul declined. He did not smoke, he said. Harry lit his pipe and said, 'Your work was adequately thorough, Dr. Saul. Have you told your patient?'

Saul shook his head. 'I wasn't all that sure. Now I am. He's on borrowed time.'

Harry nodded, puffing. 'In your view is there any need for additional talk of surgery?'

Saul shook his head. 'None, Doctor; unless it were our intention to expedite the inevitable.'

Norman Belden laid the reports aside looking vinegary. 'Damned shame the man wasn't brought here a couple of years ago. Or even five years, for the matter of that.'

Saul glanced at Belden as he'd done before; with more curiosity than interest. Then he said to Harry, 'I believe he'll wish to go home to die.'

Harry nodded again. 'Of course.' He removed the pipe. 'But perhaps it wouldn't do any harm if we kept him here a week or two doing what can be done to increase his strength. I don't know what his normal diet is, but I'd guess it hasn't been the most suitable.' Harry tapped the reports Norman had tossed back on the desk.

Saul pondered, then agreed, but Norman Belden looked at Harry as though he were something of an idiot. He did not, however, say anything until Harry had shown Geoffrey Saul out, patted the smaller man's shoulder and said they would meet again. Then Norman said, 'It can't do Memorial any good, Harry, having that man die here.'

'He may not die here, Norman.'

'May not? He could die this afternoon or tomorrow and you know it.'

For the first time Harry's restraint slipped a little. He put the pipe aside, thrust both hands deep into trouser pockets and faced the tall, thin man. 'It's all right to be a zealot,' he said, looking Belden squarely in the eye, 'as long as it doesn't interfere with facts, Norman. This is a hospital, not a political arena; our first obligation is to the people who come here to be helped. Whether we can do much, or, as in

43

this case, practically nothing, doesn't alter that. We are here to help *people*. As for that old man, we'll keep him here if he chooses to stay, do what we can ... and if he dies, he won't be the first who's done so at Memorial. As for your fears of political or public repercussions—forget it. We know what we're doing is right.'

Belden took all that with quite good grace, but a moment later, standing near the door with his hatchet-face turned, he said, 'Doctor—this does not resolve the other thing we discussed.'

Harry's restraint slipped a little further. 'I am perfectly aware of that, Doctor. Standing here and talking about it isn't going to help much either.'

'All right; what do you propose doing? The Board of Renewal will convene in six weeks.'

To Harry that last sounded like a threat. It would be the second such threat he'd had hurled at him lately on the same subject. He controlled his rising hostility with an effort and said, 'That gives us six weeks to find the answer, then, doesn't it?'

After Dr. Belden had departed, Harry sat down behind his desk, wondering again, for perhaps the hundredth time, why he'd ever given up the professorship to come to Memorial as Assistant Chief Consultant, second in command of the huge complex only to Dr. Albert Branch, when, if he'd remained at the surgeons' college he'd never have had to face any of the difficulties which were endemic in this bustling place.

Of course the answer lay in himself; he lacked Norman Belden's merciless drive and relentless ambition; he wasn't as dedicated as Albert Branch; he most certainly did not possess the Old Man's ego. But he had felt stifled, too, under the protective, sheltering roof of the college. He hadn't wanted to live and eventually die without ever having tested himself against the world.

He made a face; he was definitely testing himself now, or, perhaps more accurately, the world was testing him.

When the telephone rang he reached for it expecting Branch. It was Regina, not Albert, Branch. She said, 'I wasn't sure whether you'd want me to contact you at the hospital.' He told her it was quite all right; he had a private line in any case. She said, 'I realise you must be terribly busy; that you want to be left alone in the evenings, but—do you suppose we could meet somewhere tonight?'

It had a definitely clandestine ring to it. He smiled at himself; she was a child. 'Of course. Suppose I meet you in front of the house at the south corner of your square at seven this evening?'

'Perfect,' she said, and rang off, leaving him wandering what exactly, they were to discuss. Not in general terms, of course, he already knew what that would be, but in particular. He didn't have more than a few moments to speculate about it.

Dr. Branch walked in with only a token knock on the door, nodded and dropped into a chair. He looked tired, which he very likely was; being Chief Consultant entailed much, much more than just an occasional bout in the operating theatre. 'Well,' he said, 'you've read the results of the tests by now.'

Harry nodded.

'It would just finish the old fellow off to open him up.'

'Yes. His physician was in here; he agreed with that. Of course there is still the patient himself. He may not agree.'

That was such a remote possibility that Dr. Branch made a gesture as though annoyedly to brush any such contingency aside. 'He's in no shape to agree or disagree.' The older man fell to studying Harry's silver-filigreed pen. 'I'm glad,' he murmured. He looked glad, too. 'Even if the damned malignancy hadn't been so massive, that old man couldn't stand surgery without a lot of building-up, and even then ...' Dr. Branch shrugged. 'Sclerosis, bad pump, you name it, it's either already gone wrong inside the old lad or is about to. I wonder how old he is ?'

Harry looked surprised. 'It gives his age in the reports, sir.'

'Oh hell,' snorted the Old Man. 'That's

ridiculous. Sixty-five? Why that man's at least seventy-five—maybe eighty-five.' He raised sunken eyes to Harry's face. 'Once, years before you came here, they brought me an Eskimo with a crushed back. He said he was forty. By my tests he was at least sixty. I asked him how he knew he was forty. He grinned at me and said, 'That's how old I want to be.' At least he was honest about it. I think our African doesn't want to be older than sixty-five.'

Harry smiled. He'd encountered that situation a few times too, and not always among aboriginal peoples who made no notes of the passing years. No one really liked passing forty, and as far as women were concerned, even forty had a ring of doom to it.

Of course, the old man sitting across the desk from Harry had the identical trouble, but a relentless civilisation had pegged his birth-date, had made it public property; thanks to civilisation's enormous preoccupation with dates and years and calendars, poor Albert Branch was being for ever reminded—and thereby underminded—by a very unkind, and impersonally vindictive, society that he was an old man.

But if that fact stood, unaltered and unalterable, the other problem had quietly and neatly dissolved. There would be no crisis over the African. Harry leaned back and felt relieved. But he just was not so easily deluded.

47

As he regarded Dr. Branch sitting opposite to him, he knew perfectly well that another crisis would soon arise, and sooner or later there would be no way to sidestep.

He arose and said, 'Won't you join me downstairs over a cup of coffee, sir?'

Old Branch arose without enthusiasm, saying, 'Pleased to, Harry. Actually, what I need is stronger than caffeine, but I don't suppose you'd hold for that.'

Harry didn't answer; he didn't have to. He simply laughed it off and held the door for the older man to pass out of his office first.

CHAPTER SIX

A SECRET MEETING

A man would have had to be constructed of stone not to have been impressed by Regina at any time, but that particular night when Harry met her in what amounted almost to sinister circumstances, she looked more lovely than ever.

Of course the colour in her cheeks was due to the high, chilly wind that blew, and when she got into the car her perfume only heightened a sensation of something wonderfully clandestine.

Evidently she felt some of this too, because

she shot Harry a confused, darting look and said speaking swiftly and slightly breathlessly, 'I had to escape from Andrew, who was drearily sitting round waiting for Uncle Albert to arrive home. It made me feel like a conspirator.'

He was sympathetic even though he smiled at her. 'I circled the square twice as though shaking off some sinister pursuers. You know, Regina, I don't think either of us would make very successful spies or anarchists, or whatever.' He headed the car into town. Wind buffeted them occasionally, giving the car a hard shove or making it yaw like a small boat in a rough sea. 'Keep watch out at the back,' he admonished. 'If you see 007's car back there let me know.'

She laughed.

Of course that changed everything; the confusion, self-awareness, even the ultimate seriousness of what this was all about.

He enquired whether she'd eaten and she had. He had too, at his flat. He had a woman who came daily and although he swore she did absolutely nothing all day but read his magazines and watch the telly, he never said a word because when she left his supper each evening it was an epicurean delight.

Eventually, as he drove against the wind, he had to face an odd fact; he was quite at a loss. He couldn't, most certainly, return with Regina to his office at Memorial. It would look much worse if they went to some little lane and parked—and of course a constable would come; they always did come along when people were trying their damnedest to be discreetly unobserved. They couldn't just keep for ever driving round and round; it was difficult to talk when one was concentrating on traffic. He finally said, 'I'm sorry about this and I don't want you to misunderstand, but we'll go to my flat.'

Immediately he'd said it, heard the play-back inside his head, he blushed furiously. She was watching his profile; he knew that without looking. She said nothing at all, and of course that made the awkwardness more noticeable.

Then he made the most splendid blunder of them all. He turned with a smile and said, 'I'm old enough to be your father.'

She finally spoke. 'Well ... whether you have that distinction or not, Doctor, you certainly lack his tact.' He was astonished. Dismay he might have expected, even maidenly trepidation, but biting sarcasm, never. He decided to say nothing more and since they were approaching the block of flats where he lived he was saved from the need for breaking that resolution.

After he'd parked the car and led her inside to the lift where the wind couldn't reach them, he removed his hat. Of all the apparel men were slaves to, he had for hats the most loathing of all.

His flat, on the second floor, was actually very comfortable and commodious. Because he was fond of music he had an expensive stereophonic system with concealed speakers. As he took her coat and saw her turn slowly, studying the place, he said, 'I'm going to have a spot of brandy, can't I get you something?'

She turned to face him. 'No, thank you.'

'Warm you up,' he coaxed, and she responded with a small smile.

'That wouldn't be very suitable, would it, Doctor—giving alcohol to a minor?'

He lost most of his warm little grin. She was being sarcastic again. Well, he hadn't meant to annoy her by saying he was old enough to be her father. It'd actually been meant to allay any fears a young girl might have. He excused himself and went to the kitchen to get his brandy. Round the partition he said, 'Hadn't your uncle arrived home by the time you left to meet me?'

'No. But quite often he's late for dinner.'

Harry could believe that. He could also speculate on the peril of continued meetings between them; he'd narrowly escaped being caught the other time.

He finished pouring the brandy and went to stand in the partition-opening to look at her. She was still standing near the sofa, tallish and high-breasted, with an Achilles tendon like steel. Beautiful.

'Andrew . . . ?' he said, probing.

51

'Probably to argue. That's about all he comes round for any more. He's Uncle Albert's conscience; he told me that himself. He said you apparently were some variety of Victorian hero who'd die rather than compromise with a ridiculous principle.'

Harry strode into the sitting-room, waved her to the sofa and took a chair, leaned back with his brandy and sipped it. He was finding it increasingly difficult to view her as a fellow-conspirator. When she crossed her legs and looked at him with a soft little rueful smile, he had to remind himself: *Act your age!*

He said, 'I'm fond of him too.'

That's what made her smile. 'He's really quite nice, Dr. Blaydon. It's just that . . . well . . . he's one of those people who always has to brood. If it isn't about bombs falling on Hanoi, it's the resurgence of nationalism in Germany, but of course lately it's been Uncle Albert. He comes round at least twice a week to try and get me to tell him how much scotch Uncle Albert's drinking. I don't tell him, of course, but Uncle Albert usually does. Then Andrew is all upset.'

He brushed Andrew aside by relating to her what had occurred respecting the African politician. He didn't leave out a thing, not even Norman Belden's angry words. She seemed to wither a little on the sofa as he spoke. Afterwards she was sombre again, as she'd been when he'd picked her up in his car.

Sombre and anxious.

'It's terrible, isn't it?' she said. 'After we were together the last time—I couldn't sleep. It's a frightful way to repay all he's done for me, Dr. Blaydon. Sometimes I think Andrew is far more honest; at least he's out in the open with his thoughts.'

Harry finished the brandy. It burnt pleasantly in his belly. Nothing quite like brandy to warm a man on a bleak winter night. Unless of course it was something as disturbingly exquisite as the girl opposite him. He cleared his throat, wrenched himself into a different position like a man being punished, and said, 'Recriminations later, Regina. Now—what do you have in mind?'

'The amount he is drinking, Doctor Blaydon. I know where every bottle of it is.'

He nodded, not exactly comprehending but willing to listen. Her lips were heavy and ripe with a centre fullness.

'I can deprive him of it any afternoon. But he'll also have some at the hospital. That's where you come in.'

Harry slowly scowled. 'You expect me to go like a common thief and rummage his desk?'

She looked at him with a hardness in her eyes. 'Doctor, whose idea was all this?'

'Well, I know, Regina, but what you're saying just isn't—'

'Give me something better then, Doctor!'

He had a suggestion; had entertained it for

53

almost two weeks. But when he thought of expounding it now, it sounded just as bad as what she'd suggested. Still, he was cornered, so he said a trifle weakly, 'I believe it can be arranged for him to give a series of lectures at the college. Of course I haven't done anything about it yet, but I'm sure, if he can be persuaded, the college would be very pleased to ask him to do it.'

'Wonderful,' she breathed. 'It's so much better than my suggestion. More polished.'

Her enthusiasm pleased him but he said, 'Of course it would only be a beginning. The idea I have in mind would entail getting other engagements; it might take a year before he'd be booked up. Do you follow me?'

She nodded. 'Gradual disengagement, I believe it's called. Dr. Blaydon, you're a genius.'

'Yes,' he said, 'There's no doubt of that.' Then he laughed.

She was completely relaxed with him; whether that was flattering or not he wasn't so sure. She had a lovely neck; well set upon a supple spine. Strong, he thought; she was actually very strong physically.

'But suppose something occurs in the interim, Dr. Blaydon; it's just occurred to me that in the year we'd need, a case similar to this African's may occur again.'

That was, and he'd already realised this, the real weak link in this hypothetical chain. His

54

only response was the one he gave her. 'We'll have to face that when, and if, it arrives. In any case, I'm afraid depriving him of his liquor wouldn't prevent him from going out to a pub, would it? There will have to be calculated risks in both cases I'm afraid.' He explained that the Board of Renewal would convene within a few weeks too, which meant Andrew and Norman Belden might become additional causes for anxiety.

She finally said, 'I would like that drink now, if I'm permitted to change my mind, Dr. Blaydon.'

He went to fetch the drink, returned with it and when their hands touched as he handed it to her, she blushed. He affected not to notice, returned to his chair, crossed one leg over the other and pondered. She was twenty to his thirty-five; actually she looked no more than seventeen or eighteen and that made what he was thinking more uncomfortable to dwell upon. But she was there, ten or twelve feet away, lifesize and lovely.

He decided drinking that spot of brandy hadn't been a wise thing, everything considered.

She said, 'What are you thinking?'

It caught him off-guard. He blinked and looked guilty, and said, 'Well, of course we'll have to devise something with the Board hearings coming up, won't we?'

She gave him a long, slow, narrow-eyed

55

study over the rim of her glass before she nodded. 'I think I've heard my uncle say that a man could be flat on his back and he'd still have to go before that Board.'

He'd recovered most of his equanimity. 'That's a fair statement. Also, barring Andrew and Dr. Belden, I'm confident your uncle would sail right through. It would be somewhat ironic if he didn't, Regina; some of the tests were his own suggestions.'

She saw nothing particularly helpful there. 'Doctor, I wonder how many bullet-makers have been slain by their own products?'

He chuckled politely, but in the private part of his mind he came to a definite conclusion about Regina Barkley Branch—she was thoroughly and hard-headedly practical. Most unusual in a beautiful woman. He swung the topic back nearer to what they'd been discussing while she finished her drink, set the glass aside and turned slightly when a gust of wind struck a window, making it rattle.

'We have something like a month before the Board convenes. That really shouldn't worry us too much; if you can handle Andrew I suppose I can handle Belden. As for the lectures, I'll get on to that first thing tomorrow. That leaves a matter of time, plus ungovernable events, to be considered.'

She nodded, watching him. She seemed to be thinking of something else, or perhaps thinking along with him but on a different—

56

female—level.

'I can take care of the time, I suppose, as well as whatever arises at Memorial.'

'How?' she demanded.

'By being beside him in the operating theatre. Precisely what I've always done since going there.'

She accepted that, rose, picked up her coat, slung it over a shoulder and said, 'I feel a lot better after being with you this evening, Doctor. You have the ability to instil strength in people.' She smiled. 'You're also quite good-looking.'

That surprised him but he passed it off with a big grin. 'Strong brandy, wasn't it, Regina?'

She shook her head at him. 'Not all that strong, Doctor. Well, if you'll take me home I'll sleep more easily. Maybe this meeting wasn't even necessary, but for the past few day's I've been in desperate need of reassurance. You're the only one I can get it from, now.'

'There's Andrew,' he said, holding the door for her.

'No, there is not Andrew,' she replied with strong emphasis. 'There never was Andrew. Regardless of what my uncle may have secretly wished, or what Andrew may have wanted, Dr. Blaydon, *there has never been Andrew!*'

CHAPTER SEVEN

SOME DARK CLOUDS GATHERING

The difficulty about arranging for the lectures was not in getting the college Chairman to concur; he was delighted with the suggestion the moment Harry made it. The difficulty was in getting Dr. Branch to agree to do it.

Harry had told the Chairman, an old friend, that Dr. Branch was never to know Harry has instigated things; he would tell the Old Man the whole idea came from the college. The Chairman agreed to that but, as he had asked an obvious question, Harry had to give an honest answer.

'He is in bad need of rest. He's been at it a very long while, you know, and what he needs now is a sabbatical of sorts.'

It was the truth. Of course it wasn't all the truth and each time of late Harry'd had to indulge in that variety of mild deceit he'd flinched a little more.

He took courage from the fact that his motives were absolutely of the best. That helped. Another thing that helped was the rash of routine surgery that neither he nor his eminent colleague were called upon to participate in. It was always easiest to believe oneself right when the stress was less.

That same day he made it a point to encounter Dr. Branch in the restaurant. They lunched together. Branch looked a little morose. Harry noticed the old man being careful of his fingers as he ate. Of course that meant he'd either missed his daily injection or else he'd drunk his scotch later than usual the night before.

They discussed the African upstairs who was miraculously responding to regular hours and high-protein meals without any liquids except water. 'Tough old buzzard,' said Branch, drawing a measure of satisfaction from what the African was accomplishing. 'Except for the malignancy I should judge he'd be good for another ten years.'

Harry concurred. 'You've doubtless seen hundreds like him,' he said, then looked up suddenly. 'Have you ever considered writing a book, sir? Something like *Fifty Years In Medicine*.'

The Old Man's eyes sparkled with amusement. 'And tell the unvarnished truth? Harry, only a dedicated liar can do that without making himself appear more wrong than right. No thanks.'

For a moment they were silent, and Dr. Branch's keen eyes rested upon the younger man in thoughtful appraisal. He still wore the amused look only now it was more sardonic. Eventually he said, 'But I did have a request to do a series of lectures at your old college.'

Harry steeled himself, then looked surprised, hoping he didn't look *too* surprised; in his private opinion the actor's curse was never under-acting, it was always *overacting*.

It was impossible to tell from the Old Man's expression whether the expression of surprise was totally convincing. The Old Man said, 'Very appealing offer it was, at that.' Harry let a moment pass before saying, 'When I was over there I used to try and get qualified lecturers to come round now and then. The hell of it was, there just never were enough I thought good enough.'

Albert Branch looked steadily at the younger man. 'You never contacted me, Harry.' He smiled softly. 'Not good enough?'

'You know better, sir. But would you have come?'

'No,' said the Old Man without a moment's hesitation. 'I'm reminded of something Ernest Hemingway once said: 'Men who can write can't speak.' That's also true of surgeons, I think.'

Harry shook his head. He'd heard Dr. Branch speak many times. True, it was never at a lectern, and also true, it was to a very small, specialised audience of other surgeons. But the Old Man knew his subjects very well; he had the confidence too.

'You'd be a smashing success,' he told the old man. 'You also owe that much to the college.'

Dr. Branch sat a moment regarding the remnants of his lunch. 'The fee is surprisingly large, Harry. Tell me—did anyone over there ever contact you about asking me to do this?'

Harry was sweating. He had a premonition that Dr. Branch either knew something or suspected something. He searched for an answer and tried to make it sound light. 'I recall a discussion concerning you before I came to Memorial; someone thought you'd be the best man in the country for a series of lectures on techniques. But as I said before, the idea seemed too wildly out of reach.'

'Well,' exclaimed Dr. Branch, laying aside his napkin, 'I agreed to think it over.' He rose and reached for his pen to sign the bill a diffident waitress placed before him. Harry saw the sudden contraction of muscles around his eyes, saw the tough old lips flatten perceptibly as he bent and signed. The Old Man's hands were giving him hell today.

They parted on the fourth floor, Harry going along to his office, Dr. Branch heading in the direction of the Control Desk.

It was a quiet afternoon until two or a little after when Regina called. She said her uncle and Andrew'd had a row last night. Her uncle had come in rather late; she hadn't been there, of course, so Andrew had sat with the old man through a dinner she'd put on the stove to keep warm for him.

All she really knew was that when she got

61

home her uncle was sitting before a nice fire in the sitting-room with a great amber glass of scotch and water in front of him and Andrew had gone. Her uncle had said Andrew had ragged him for drinking again, and this time he'd hit the ceiling. They'd had words and Andrew had flung out of the house.

Of course, as he listened, Harry began to understand the Old Man's discomfort today; the whisky, as usual, negated the medication. That's why his hands were troubling him.

He tried to soothe Regina. She was distraught, but strangely, she was not the least bit angry. Even when she mentioned Andrew she sounded impersonal.

'When I'm around I can see the sparks coming and head them off. If I'd been there last night I'm sure there'd have been no fight.'

Harry wondered if she meant that as a reproach. Of course the idea of a meeting had been hers not his. Still, he'd handled enough females to know how irrational their logic could be sometimes. He said, 'I'm terribly sorry, Regina. However, if it'll make you feel any better, I had luncheon with him today and he was able to joke. But his hands are bothering him. Also, we discussed the lecture series; he seemed receptive.' Here, Harry had to be cautious; no point in raising her hopes. 'I called the college as I promised; they were perfectly willing.'

She said, 'He'll no doubt tell me about it

this evening. I'll try to get him to make a favourable decision.'

'Do that,' he said. 'Let me know if you have any luck.'

He was lighting his pipe after ringing off when Dr. Belden walked in accompanied by George Laxalt. George looked unhappy, even unwilling, but Belden was evidently in charge and Laxalt, an easy-going, poised and efficient administrator, was evidently humouring Belden.

Harry eyed them and gravely nodded. He didn't smile because he felt that this was unlikely to be a social visit. He waved them to chairs, puffed up a goodly cloud of smoke and when Norman Belden leaned forward as though to launch into one of his coldly-reasoned, eminently logical assaults, Harry forestalled him.

'The College of Surgeons wants Dr. Branch to give a series of lectures. We had lunch together; he's considering accepting.' Harry paused to watch for reaction. Laxalt looked immensely relieved. He leaned back in his chair and actually smiled. Dr. Belden, evidently caught unprepared, blinked, flicked his glance to the wall where Dr. Blaydon's certificates hung, framed, then looked back at Harry.

'Will he accept?' he asked, and of course Harry had no answer to that.

'He didn't say he would or wouldn't,

63

Norman. All he said was that he'd think about it. I take that to mean the idea isn't uninteresting to him.'

Belden eased back in his chair, shot Laxalt a look, then dropped a bombshell. 'Harry, George was informed half an hour ago that Premier Ibn Abdullah of Trans-Arabia will arrive the day after tomorrow for admittance.'

Harry's pipe-smoke dwindled down to a mere wisp, then that faded too. He removed the pipe, set it in his giant ashtray, looked squarely at Laxalt and said in what he hoped was a calm voice: 'George ...?'

Laxalt gave a little perfunctory smile. 'Norman was in the office when the call came. I didn't have a chance to have Dr. Branch informed. The Premier's physician, a Jordanian named Haroush, would only say His Excellency hasn't been up to snuff lately and wants a thorough examination. It didn't sound too dire to me, Harry.'

Laxalt's last sentence sounded slightly reproachful. He glanced at Belden, which inclined Harry towards the conclusion that Belden didn't share Laxalt's equanimity. Harry knew exactly why he did not and moved at once to spike Belden's guns.

'We wait until His Excellency's been properly examined, until we have all the reports, exactly as we did in the case of the African. That's all.'

There was a solid ring of finality in Harry's

64

voice that anyone but Norman Belden might have deferred to. Belden lifted a sheaf of curled papers from a pocket and held them out towards Harry.

'The Premier's past medical history,' he announced. 'He's been coming here every year or so for a long time. There's enough in here to prepare you for any eventualities.'

Harry received the papers but put them still rolled on his desk and kept looking squarely at Belden. 'I'm obliged,' he said, with a trace of tough irony. 'Norman, I'd have looked this up anyway, you know. As for anything else—we wait.'

Laxalt was watching them as though anticipating being called upon to arbitrate. He was very uncomfortable.

But Belden had no more ammunition, unless of course he chose to bring up the theme of the Old Man's deterioration again, and there was really no sound basis for doing that. Someone else might have; another man with more emotion might have hurled a charge, but Harry didn't expect Belden to, and Belden did not; he was not emotional. He would say exactly what he thought only when it was entirely relevant. That was his absolutely rational nature.

He rose. 'I'm late for lunch,' he said, and departed.

Laxalt fished round for a limp packet of cigarettes lit one, blew smoke and cast a pained look in Harry's direction. 'I always was under the impression one found *prima donnas* only in opera.'

Harry smiled. 'He's not a *prima donna*, George. Norman's a damned fine surgeon. But like a lot of men who've punished themselves with whips until they feel they've achieved real perfection, he's a zealot. A couple of hundred years ago he'd have ridden about the countryside slaying heretics, burning witches, that sort of thing. The trick with Norman is to keep him leashed to a damned surgical table. Otherwise he could give a man ulcers.'

'What's he got against the Old Man, Harry?'

Evidently Norman had kept his own counsel; Harry could have thanked him for that. Nothing was worse for hospital morale than for someone to undermine the Chief Consultant. Nothing at all.

All Harry said was, 'He's ambitious. You know that. Norman's tops at the trade; he also happens to aspire to great things. Personally, I believe he'll eventually achieve them. But because Albert Branch is old doesn't mean Norman's going to step into his shoes.'

Laxalt looked scandalised. 'Is that what's eating at him? Good lord; he couldn't begin to handle the Old Man's position.'

Harry rose. 'I know it. I suppose everyone who knows anything at all about Memorial knows it. Except Norman Belden. Anyway, don't spread rumours, George, and don't worry about Norman. I'll see to it that he doesn't get too far out of line.'

'I hope so,' said Laxalt, also rising. He looked as worried now as when he'd first entered the office. He managed a sickly smile, though, at the door. 'You know I was offered a tremendous position with an international accounting firm when I accepted this post. I should have my head examined.'

Harry laughed, saw his guest out, turned and regarded the papers Belden had left on his desk and said aloud, 'George, you aren't the only one who should have his damned head examined. Oh well . . .'

CHAPTER EIGHT

A SMALL TRIUMPH

The pleasant little girl on the ground floor said. 'Good night, Dr. Blaydon,' even though it wasn't quite four o'clock. Outside, though, the sky was steely, there were scudding old ragged clouds, and the wind was at it again, making it seem late in the evening.

Harry reached his flat feeling a little more anxious than usual but not especially apprehensive. He'd determined from Premier Ibn Abdullah's medical record that while there were complaints of a gastro-abdominal and intestinal nature stretching back nearly fifteen years, His Excellency actually was in surprisingly good physical shape at his last examination, about eighteen months earlier.

Harry did not suspect there would be any need for surgery and therefore his primary concern was the publicity sure to follow the Premier's arrival at Memorial, with its consequent gaggle of newsmen who were nuisances however one considered them.

He was perfectly satisfied with Memorial's examination procedures. His Excellency would be gone over with a fine-tooth comb.

Actually, after Harry had reached his flat, and had taken a shower before sitting down to his pre-prepared supper, he had pushed His Excellency into the back of his mind; there really was only one possible peril. If His Excellency required surgery, and if the Old Man performed it, and if the Old Man's hands gave out . . .

A lot of 'ifs'—perhaps too many to mean much.

Harry was thinking of Norman Belden as he ate his dinner. It was then slightly before seven in the evening but the night beyond his windows was as dark and threatening as though it were a stormy ten o'clock.

If Norman and Andrew Connell teamed up at the Board hearing there would inevitably be a scandal. It really did not matter very much what the Board decreed; what would do the

68

damage would be the publicity. Albert Branch was internationally famous; he stood upon his own private pinnacle.

There would be a few who'd be glad to see him fall, of course; he hadn't reached that eminence without treading upon some toes. But by and large the ones who would really pass judgement—after a scandal—would be the public, at home and abroad.

Harry finished eating, cleared away the dishes, lit a pipe and went to the sitting-room to read his evening paper. He first set the stereophonic system to piping music throughout the flat. Because he was a stickler, he fiddled with the controls until he had such fidelity of sound that it was as though a concert orchestra were in the very next room.

Then he sat down, flicked open the paper, and the doorbell jangled. It startled him. He peered over the top of his newspaper at the door as though it had personally affronted him. He had his share of callers, usually other medical men although he had a small circle of private acquaintances as well, but not often did people arrive unannounced; it was customary to telephone first.

He put the newspaper aside, laid the pipe in an ashtray and crossed to the door. The wind outside was moaning and a bent limb from a tree scrabbled along the outside of the building. A terrible night for going calling.

When he opened the door Regina was

standing there. She hadn't even been in his thoughts, therefore his initial reaction was one of trouble. He stepped aside for her to enter, took the coat she shed, then said, 'Is something wrong?'

She looked at him as though he'd asked a foolish question. 'Nothing that hasn't been wrong for a long time, Doctor.'

He took her to the sofa, seated her and then asked if she'd like a little something to warm her up, for although it was very cozy in the flat, she'd just come in out of a bleak and blustery night.

She shook her head. 'I can't stay very long and I'm not cold, really. Had the heater on in the car all the way.' She glanced out of a window where blackness lay, where a wild wind cried, shuddered and looked back.

I didn't want to risk telephoning you.'

Harry sat down, reached for the cooling pipe, and felt a tightness knotting his stomach. 'He's drinking tonight . . . ?'

She smiled at him. 'No, Doctor. He's decided to accept the college's offer to undertake a series of lectures.'

Harry, braced for the worst, had the feeling of a man who'd been leaning against a door which had suddenly given way. He held the pipe in his hand as he looked at her, then slowly leaned back and slowly smiled. 'You scared hell out of me,' he said.

She laughed. 'I was afraid that might be

your reaction when I came banging on the door. But he's got a couple of old cronies at the house tonight and I was afraid that if I telephoned you, he might inadvertently hear. I wanted to get word to you so I lied to him. I said I was going to the pictures.' She pulled her lovely mouth down in a pout of distaste. 'I suppose it's inevitable that deceit, even when indulged in to protect or help someone, makes one a liar.'

He could have disputed that. Most certainly he could have disputed her complex of guilt, but all he said was, 'You are far too lovely ever to be disreputable whatever the reason. Are you sure I couldn't at least get you some tea?'

She shook her head, regarded him silently for a moment then rose. 'I've said all I came to say.' She went over where he'd placed her coat and reached for it. He sprang up at once to assist.

She looked at him over her shoulder. 'What is next, Doctor? Will he be required to live at the college while giving his series of lectures?'

'Not at all. In fact he can commute from home and back with less inconvenience than he now has to put up with in reaching Memorial.'

She turned. 'And of course you will assume the position of the chief consultant while he's at the college?'

Harry nodded. 'On an acting basis. He will remain chief. All important decisions will still be his to make.'

She looked up into his eyes. 'Doctor, what happens when the Board of Renewal convenes?'

'Well, of course he'll be called up, but I would imagine he'd have no trouble. Providing of course Connell and Belden don't appear.' He smiled. 'If you'll see to it Connell learns of the lecture series, I'll see that Belden also hears. That should alleviate most of the pressure.'

'But the lectures,' she asked. 'How long will they last? They won't keep him away from the operating theatre for more than a few months, will they?'

'At the college, no, but if you and I can achieve a respite of several months I'm positive we can arrange additional lecture series.' He felt as confident as he sounded and looked. 'Give him a year on the lecture circuit, Regina, and I'm fairly sure we'll have engineered an agreeable transition for him.'

He didn't come right out and say that within a year it was highly probable Dr. Branch's illness would be pronounced enough so that even he would have to accept the finality and imminence of retirement, at least from active surgery. However, that was what was in his mind as he took her elbow and steered her towards the door. But she halted and said her uncle had mentioned something about a distinguished patient arriving soon at

72

Memorial. He explained about the Premier of Trans-Arabia then said, 'He is not young and he has a history of intestinal trouble. Nothing serious as far as his record goes.' He patted her shoulder and leaned to open the door. 'I'll see your uncle about the man in the morning. I hope he confirms what you've told me about the lecture-series.' He hadn't opened the door but was ready to.

She said, with what appeared to be a little self-conscious smile, 'I know I'm being foolish, Doctor, but I have an odd feeling that things are going too smoothly.'

He understood the feeling. 'If there's a black cloud round the corner we shall deal with it when it appears. Good night, Regina, and thanks awfully for coming round.

After he'd closed the door, he leaned upon it. This night he'd had no brandy—in fact his recent and heavy dinner was lying like soggy lead in his stomach—and he'd still felt that quickening of the pulse and spirit with her.

'No fool like an old fool,' he told himself sternly, went back to his pipe and newspaper, and frowned so hard it interfered with his reading.

Then the mood passed, he finished the paper, lay his pipe aside, hooked both arms behind his head and sat slouched, looking at the ceiling.

Of course there were some likely pitfalls between this initial lecture engagement and

73

whatever came afterwards, but progress had most certainly been made, a respite had been achieved, and if he worked as diligently at getting more lectures set up, and if *she* could muzzle that insufferable pup, Andrew Connell, it all just might come out right after all.

He went to bed feeling almost satisfied with himself. He awoke the same way, arrived at Memorial at seven in the morning and went at once to the restaurant, his habitual routine since—and he made no secret of it—he was as helpless as a child in a kitchen. He had once told George Laxalt, an old married man, that alleged connubial bliss aside, cooking was probably the predominant factor in bachelordom that ultimately drove single men into wedlock.

Norman Belden was just ahead of him. They nodded then Norman waited, reserving a place at a small table in the noisy, very crowded room. Harry went over without much enthusiasm, smiled his appreciation and sat down. A hovering waitress pounced. They ordered, then looked about. Most of the other members of Memorial, both male and female, who had no one at home to prepare breakfast, were also in the room. Fortunately the restaurant was large.

Belden said, 'There is a rumour that the Old Man may go on the lecture circuit, Harry. Heard anything about it?'

'Only that he may talk at the college,

74

Norman.'

Their food came. Belden started eating. He ate an awful lot for a stringy, gangling man with no fat on his frame. He said, between mouthfuls, 'It would be exactly right, if he'd do it and if he'd go right on doing it for the rest of his active life, don't you think?'

Harry looked up. 'I'm just trying to have my breakfast, Norman, not get all wound up in the affairs of other people. Do you mind?'

Belden blushed, lifted a cup and said no more.

Actually, doctors Blaydon and Belden had never been close friends. They had managed to remain acquaintances despite their frequent co-operation in the operating theatre. They had very little in common; even their approaches to their profession were different.

Harry never would have voluntarily eaten breakfast at the same table with Norman Belden. As a matter of fact there were not very many members of the staff who would have.

While almost everyone respected Belden's efficiency and his dedication, the same people deplored him otherwise.

George Laxalt, passing through, having already eaten, looked, then looked again. Harry saw that double-take but Norman missed it. Laxalt was surprised at seeing them sharing the same table.

Upstairs, later on in the morning, when Harry met Laxalt, the accountant said, 'Very

75

agreeable twosome you two made in the restaurant.'

Harry smiled. 'Have you tried eating in a corner, cross-legged lately, George? It was there or the floor.'

Laxalt grinned. 'It's a clean floor.' Then he passed on to the next thing uppermost in his mind. 'Dr. Branch requisitioned all the reports on Ibn Abdullah. He didn't behave as if he were impressed.'

Harry could understand that. 'Unless the old boy's come loose somewhere else, the reports from years past would lead one to suspect he's not in very bad shape.'

'The Old Man said if I ran across you, Harry, I was to tell you he'd like you to call in at his office, if you have the time.'

Harry had the time. As a matter of fact he had nothing arranged until the following morning. He returned to his own office first, for his pipe, then went along to the Chief Consultant's office. There, encountering the grey-haired but very handsome and well-preserved woman who had been serving as Dr. Branch's private secretary for fifteen years, he said, 'Emily, he wanted to see me.'

The handsome woman nodded. 'Go in now, Harry. He's having a cup of tea; at this time he's always ready for visitors.' She smiled.

Harry studied the smile, wondering if Emily, who was very keen and alert, had noticed any deterioration in her private hero. He said,

'Thanks,' and headed for the nearby closed door, thinking that even if Emily had noticed, she'd be the last person on earth to say anything, and that made him sigh exactly as he'd had occasion to sigh over the dangerous loyalty of Regina Barkley Branch. It wasn't just a question of loyalty, it was also a question of contributing to a great man's ruin, and perhaps contributing also to some poor devil's unecessary death.

CHAPTER NINE

A TOUCH OF TEMPER

The imminence of His Arabic Excellency's appearance at Memorial held Dr. Branch's interest only quite briefly as he tapped the folder on his desk for Harry's benefit.

'One of those dehydrated old mummies who live to be a hundred,' he said. 'He's had duodenal ulcers from time to time. I rather imagine, from what I've read in the newspapers, the old boy's been entitled to 'em, what with coups and counter-coups always in process in his oil-domain. Must be a hell of an existence, not knowing whether your personal servant or your bodyguard has been got at by the opposition. Care for some tea, Harry?'

'No thank you,' replied Blaydon. 'I ate an

hour ago. Incidentally, I shared a table with Norman Belden. He said he'd heard you were about to embark upon a distinguished career as a lecturer.'

Dr. Branch laughed. 'Nothing would please him more. Of course he knows about the arthritis. I would imagine he can visualise himself holding court in your office while you move in here.' The Old Man's smile lingered but there wasn't much of it reflected in the hawkish, grey eyes. 'Belden's the kind of man who keeps everyone else on their toes, eh? He's a perfectionist—which I admire—but he's also a sorry excuse for a *man*, and that I can't admire. Well it takes all kinds, doesn't it?'

'Yes, sir, it certainly does.'

'As for the lecture—yes—I was on the 'phone to the college this morning. Details will have to be worked out; after all, while I can do with a rest, I won't give up here at Memorial. You'll be acting for me, Harry. Will you mind that?'

'No, sir, not at all. And if anything comes up you should know about, believe me if I have to rout you out at midnight, you'll hear of it.'

Dr. Branch finished his tea, pushed the cup aside and glanced absently at his wrist watch. 'By the way, Regina's coming down to have luncheon with me. Would you join us?'

Harry nodded, murmuring that he'd be delighted to, but he had a little uneasy sensation between the shoulders.

78

He was almost positive it sprang from a sense of guilt; by now if the Old Man suspected anything he'd have let Harry know. He wasn't sly nor devious, but rather, was very blunt and direct.

'I'll leave Mr. Ibn Abdullah to you when he arrives tomorrow, Harry. I've got to go over to the college. The examinations would be routine anyway, I should imagine.'

'Exactly.'

'One other thing; I have to go and see the governors this afternoon—let them know what I'm planning to do. That will leave Regina on her own; I was wondering if you'd entertain her for a while, until I return? I should be through by six o'clock.'

'I'd be happy to,' Harry said, and he meant it. He *would* be happy to entertain Regina.

Dr. Branch glanced at his wrist again. 'Anything else, Harry?'

No, sir.'

Then maybe one of us had better get back on the floor, eh?'

Harry took his leave, winked at Dr. Branch's handsome secretary as he strolled out of the silent, airy office, and started back to his own room.

Of course Memorial's Board of Governors might object to Dr. Branch taking this sabbatical, as it were, in order to launch himself as a lecturer, but it wasn't very likely; ordinarily, hospital governors were delighted

79

to have their staff members called upon to speak. It was good for public-relations.

This time, the governors wouldn't have an inkling anyone was pulling strings behind the scene to keep the Old Man lecturing. Maybe, if things worked out as Harry prayed they might, the governors would eventually protest, but that was one of those 'dark clouds' Harry'd meant when he'd told Regina, the evening before, they'd face them when they arrived.

Arriving at his office, Harry got a distinct surprise. George Laxalt was inside with a stocky, swarthy man with a beautiful set of very even, very white teeth, who shoved a strong hand at Harry saying, 'I'm Premier Ibn Abdullah's personal physician, Dr. Blaydon—Dr. Saud Haroush.'

Harry gripped the extended hand, smiled, and shot Laxalt a look. George lifted and dropped his shoulders. 'We just came up,' he said, looking as though it had all been taken out of his hands. 'Emily, from Doctor Branch's office, said you'd just left there. Didn't bother to have you informed of our arrival, Harry.'

It wasn't any great breach of etiquette anyway, and Harry, once recovered from his surprise, stepped round to the chair behind his desk and smiled at Dr. Haroush, who was a man of perhaps forty-five but who looked ten years younger. Also, Haroush had a very open and friendly smile.

'I didn't think you'd be arriving today,' said

Harry, and the Arab physician spread his arms. 'His Excellency was able to get away one day early. We arrived last night, in fact. His Excellency has protocol to observe today, so he still won't come to the Memorial Hospital until tomorrow.' Haroush smiled broadly. 'But I—well—I am simply a physician; simply one member of the entourage, you see, and since no one is sick from drinking too much— because we landed here at midnight last night—no one needed me, and I thought I'd come down on my own.'

Saud Haroush spoke perfect English, which was not surprising since most prominent Middle-Easterners were educated in either Britain or the United States. He dressed as a Westerner too, and even had the mannerisms, as when he offered his hammered-silver cigarette case around, and afterwards lit up alone—and the aroma was of tobacco, not incense, which meant the cigarette was also of Western manufacture.

He had jet-black eyes that sparkled with wit. His personality was open, friendly, magnetic. Harry Blaydon felt himself coming under the man's spell and made no effort to resist. He asked how His Excellency's health was and Dr. Haroush looked bland.

'Good; His Excellency is, for a man his age, in fine health. The trouble is, you see, he doesn't believe it. Whenever he doesn't think he should be healthy, he complains of stomach pains.' Haroush rolled his handsome black eyes. 'Well, I take his orders. If he doesn't think he should be healthy, then I recommend we come here and have him examined.' Haroush clapped both hands together and grinned. 'What is it . . .? A prophet is without honour in his own country? Gentlemen, I have three degrees, but you see His Excellency secretly declines to believe a countryman of his can be as astute as British or American doctors.' Haroush dropped grey ash into Harry's large ashtray.

For Harry it was amusing. He said, 'His Excellency's records show a kind of chronic gastro upset, Doctor.'

Haroush immediately nodded. 'Absolutely. And if either of you ate what he does, I promise you'd have a perforated stomach. But for the past four years I've had control over his diet. It's not bland—he'd have my throat cut for that—but it's bland by *our* standards.' Haroush arose. 'If he has anything wrong with his inside, gentlemen, I'll eat my hat!'

Harry and George grinned as they arose. Harry said, 'I wouldn't want to see you have to do that, Doctor. When will His Excellency be round? Tomorrow morning?'

'Early, I'm afraid. He's a very early riser and has little patience with those who are not. Therefore, I apologise in advance. We'll probably appear at seven in the morning.'

George blinked. Memorial was of course a

twenty-four hour institution, but the daytime staff ordinarily didn't assume duties until seven. Harry took them out into the hall, assuring Dr. Haroush he and the others who would have to deal with Ibn Abdullah, would be at hand when he arrived.

Harry was still softly smiling when Dr. Branch called to say Regina and he would meet Harry in the restaurant in fifteen minutes. Harry had to glance at his watch to believe that half the day was already gone. It was.

Norman Belden took the lift down with Harry. They spoke a little; Harry told of Ibn Abdullah's physician's visit. Dr. Belden listened closely and eventually shrugged.

'Hypochondriacs,' he said dryly, 'are usually filtered out before they get here.'

Harry smiled. 'Unless they happen to be Premiers of oil sheikdoms, Norman,' and Belden allowed himself to come as close to a smile as he ever did when he replied.

'Precisely.'

When they reached the restaurant it was already crowded with those taking an early lunch. Dr. Branch and Regina were sitting at his private corner table. Regina looked up and smiled as Harry approached. He smiled back. She looked more beautiful than ever, or perhaps, as he told himself, it might all be a matter of lighting. The last couple of times he'd seen her it had been dark.

Dr. Branch started to get up, but Harry swiftly slid into a chair so that the older man wouldn't have to bother. The Old Man said, 'You remember Regina, Harry.'

With a gentle smile and a direct look Harry said, 'I never could have forgotten her, sir.'

Branch looked swiftly at Blaydon, then at his niece, then resumed eating. He and Regina had already been served. When the waitress came Harry gave her his order and Regina waited until that was over to say, 'You haven't changed at all, Dr. Blaydon.'

She was laughing at him. He accepted it in good humour. But you have, Regina. You must be ten pounds heavier.'

She blushed and the Old Man looked startled. He squinted at the two of them for a moment before Emily came over to whisper in his ear, distracting him. Regina took advantage of that interlude to scowl darkly. Harry's eyes twinkled in silent amusement.

After Emily had departed Dr. Branch said, 'I've already explained to Queenie that I'll be off on business for a while this afternoon, Harry, and that you'll take over for me at entertaining her.'

Regina said, 'I don't think I ought to impose on Dr. Blaydon, Uncle Albert. I'll just drive on home and—'

'Nonsense,' said Harry quickly. 'It's no imposition. I'll show you round and all the young housemen will think you're my

84

daughter.'

It was the wrong thing to say but neither Harry nor the Old Man knew it until Regina put down her fork, turned slightly pale and glared at Harry. 'Dr. Blaydon, I'm well into my twenties. Believe me, no one could ever mistake you for being my father!'

Dr. Branch sat agape staring at his docile niece. Harry, still wearing half a smile, felt it freeze on his face; then he felt blood rushing into his cheeks from the sting of her tone.

'I'm terribly sorry,' he murmured. 'Regina, I didn't mean any offence.'

She looked at both of them. 'I'm sick and tired of being treated as a child!'

Dr. Branch said, 'All right, Queenie, all right. No one shall treat you as one hereafter. Now come along and finish your lunch.' He looked helplessly over at Harry, trying to convey some kind of silent apology. Harry smoothed it all over by genially winking back, and they all fell to eating again.

Several tables away three youthful housemen were alternately ogling Regina and speaking in avid, low whispers. Harry was aware of all this, was certain Regina was also conscious of it, and he did not for a moment blame the young men. She was, far and away, the most beautiful woman in the restaurant.

Eventually Dr. Branch looked at his watch, heaved a resigned sigh and put his napkin aside as he prepared to rise. 'Take care, you two,' he said, smiling at them both. 'Queenie, now please don't be disagreeable. Harry's doing me a favour.' He winked at Dr. Blaydon and rose, straightened his coat and marched off. At once Regina raised her eyes in a mischievous little smile.

'I apologise for being a poor sport, Doctor. I started it by teasing you, then I couldn't take it when you teased back.'

'I'll survive,' said Harry dryly. 'But for a moment I wasn't sure that you were teasing. Would you prefer strolling through Memorial, or would you rather trust to luck and let me take you for a drive?'

'A drive where?'

Harry shook his head. 'No warnings in advance. After all, you're a grown woman now. Take your chances like grown women should.'

She nodded. 'Lead off, Doctor.'

CHAPTER TEN

KISSED BY A WOMAN NOT A GIRL!

It had been some time since he'd gone down to Leeswold; in fact the last time had been the first meeting he'd had with Regina, and that had been in early autumn, while it was now past Christmas. On the way they talked a little of the successful *ploy* Harry had accomplished.

86

She said her uncle had actually been going over some old notes in his study and working up a series of lectures.

'I actually think he's looking forward to it,' she said.

Harry was pleased on that score. There were still the pitfalls but he didn't drag them up; he felt there'd be plenty of time if, and when, they actually occurred. He told her of Dr. Haroush, making her smile. He also said he wouldn't dare take her back to Memorial because those enterprising young housemen would probably mob her.

She had a quiet little amused laugh for that, and a smooth reply. 'Boys, Doctor. They're boys, and you can believe me when I say boys are harmless. All toes and stammers.'

He drove into the village wearing a slow, tolerant little smile over her last remark. She probably hadn't meant it to sound sophisticated but it had, and that amused him because he still felt very ancient in comparison with her.

It was difficult to remember that she really was over twenty-one; she didn't look quite eighteen.

He thought of taking her to The Gargoyle but he might not have even considered it, respectable though the pub was, except for her recent adult attitude.

He drew up in front of the inn, heard the noise inside where the people were, and watched her profile. She looked first at the horrible old weather-worn sign of a gargoyle, then at the not-exactly-natty exterior of the building. It was old, stone, damp-looking as though perhaps Leeswold had recently had rain, and it seemed hardly modern, which of course it wasn't. Then she looked at him. He climbed out, stepped round to her side and held the door. As she stood up beside him she said, 'Quaint, Doctor. Very quaint.' He controlled his amusement until she dropped her eyes, then he smiled in spite of himself.

'Ugly,' he suggested. 'Isn't that what quaint means, Regina?'

He took her indoors and at once a heavy silence ensued. He knew the men in there, a rough, friendly lot, and they knew him, but they were far less curious about his long absence than they were about the beautiful girl on his arm. They unabashedly stared.

He winked at the publican and made his long-absent gesture for drinks to be served all round. The publican nodded and went to work while Harry steered Regina to a smoky old corner where a worn oak table with an uneven leg stood.

'I can almost see the soldiers returning through the doorway,' she murmured, looking enchanted.

He said, 'Which war?'

'Oh, Napoleonic at least.'

When their beer came he held the glass

aloft, twisted and looked at the silent men ranged elsewhere in the room. 'To a short winter and a warm spring, Gentlemen!'

They responded at once, several of them grinning evilly at him.

Regina said, 'Why do you like this place so, Doctor? I mean—it's awfully picturesque and all . . .'

He downed half his beer, set the glass down and said,

A woman would know why I like Leeswold. A girl wouldn't but a woman would.'

Her expression underwent a slow, slow change as she studied his face in the mellow half-light of the old room. She said, 'Because it's very old and comfortable. Because it's earthy and—well—coarse, the way men sometimes like things.'

He looked at his glass of old and mild, which was a very dark, almost chocolatey, brown. 'Because it's home, Queenie.'

'You said it wasn't your village.'

'I never had a village. I had a city and who the hell ever took the pulse of a city? Leeswold is a love, a mate, a mother and father.' He finished the beer, held the glass in his heavy fist and said. 'You've a bit to learn before you're really a woman.'

The colour began climbing; her blue eyes began slowly to darken as her face paled, her lips flattened. He read all the signs and smiled at them.

'Woman enough,' she whispered to him, and leaned towards him. 'You could have taken me walking through the hospital, Harry, but you had something else in mind. All right I'm here, and I'm woman enough.'

He stiffened where he sat. A slight feeling of bewilderment mixed with panic stirred in him. The publican came over with a pair of fresh glasses, removed his empty one—she'd scarcely touched hers yet—and impassively returned behind his bar.

'Drink,' said Harry Blaydon. 'You're woman enough, Regina, I'll concede that. Drink what you want and let's drive on, down to the stream.'

He wanted to get out of the inn before she did, or said, something that would be heard or seen by those motionless spectators behind them.

She sipped her beer, grimaced, rose and said, 'I never cared for the stuff,' then, as though anticipating something, she added, 'Nor scotch either.'

No one said a word as they walked out into the steely afternoon again and got into his car. Harry looked a trifle grim as he switched on the ignition and pulled away.

She reached, touched his cheek, and said, 'I came near to embarrassing you, didn't I? Well, you're lucky, because I came near to doing something that most certainly would have given your friends back there something to talk about.'

She didn't say what that was and he didn't ask. They took a left lane from the centre of Leeswold, wound down a somewhat abruptly winding by-road and eventually came to a wide place with a sparkling little stream just ahead. He pulled up and switched off the engine. Across the stream what may have once been a toll-taker's cottage stood under a slaty sky with ivy climbing all across its front. The whole scene would have made a wonderful painting.

He turned on his seat, 'You've got a lot of your uncle in you, young lady . . . excuse me: young *woman*. It's a perverse streak.' He wasn't angry but he no longer smiled so readily either.

She did; she seemed to smile with a more personal meaning to it than before. 'Harry, how old are you? Uncle Albert guessed thirty-five. I guessed thirty-two.'

He affected surprise. 'You didn't ask Andrew to guess?'

He'd stung her again and saw it in the momentary darkening of her soft eyes. 'I told you before, Harry, Andrew was never any more than he is now.'

He had no wish to explore that topic so he said, 'Your uncle was right; thirty-five. The other statistics are six feet tall and the weight is . . .'

'Is fourteen years difference in our ages such an impassable gulf, Harry?'

He flushed. 'What are you talking about?' He knew perfectly well what she was talking about. He also knew that he'd entertained some pretty unique thoughts, for him, about her as well. But at the moment he was uncomfortable and wished only to discover a way to extricate himself. 'Fourteen years is a long while, Regina. A child can almost become a man in that length of time—or a woman.' He licked his lips. 'Furthermore, your uncle wouldn't approve of . . .'

'Stop it,' she said softly, and leaned forward as she'd done back at the pub, only this time she kept on leaning until their faces were inches apart, then she kissed him.

He felt awkwardly out of his element, but the touch of her lips, the fragrance of her hair, the light riffle of breath upon his cheeks, overcame all that. He reached, caught her by the upper arms and pulled her still closer.

When they drew apart she said, 'I'm a hussy. I told my uncle I'd have to be, to do it.'

He leaned his head back, rolled it and looked at her. 'Regina, this isn't fair to you. You'd be so much better off with someone nearer your own age. Believe me it's not fair . . . to you.'

She was smiling at him, cheeks slightly flushed, eyes like blue-white diamonds, tiny teeth showing between parted lips. 'Do you want to know what my uncle told me?'

He nodded.

'He told me you'd become very proper, very aloof, very much the professional man. His exact words were—Harry, don't get angry—"Stuffed shirt".'

He slowly sat up. 'You and your uncle have discussed me in this—this light, Regina?'

She nodded. 'When I came to your flat last night I wasn't really obliged to. Didn't you guess that?'

'Well, you said you couldn't have telephoned.'

She smiled at him. 'And *you* called *me* the child. But that's true, I couldn't have telephoned. Only I didn't have to come at all, Harry. Uncle Albert would have told you he was going to give the lectures this morning at the hospital.' Her smile lingered. 'And you took me to the door.'

He felt himself turning scarlet, and tried a weak defence.

I didn't think I should keep you there on such a frightful night.

'Nor perhaps take me home, either . . .'

'You had your car.'

She laughed at him, raised both arms and put her hands on his shoulders. 'Anyway, Uncle Albert said I might have to be bold. He didn't like the word—hussy.'

Harry gently perspired. He was trapped in the car. He felt like climbing out and taking a vigorous walk along the road, or down the back of the stream. He knew something she didn't know: She'd just tied him in knots. He'd resolutely refused to permit himself to think of her as being desirable.

'Lord,' he groaned. 'Regina, I was in love with you the first time we talked—here in Leeswold. But it was just too—too fantastic. Here I am, thirty-five years old, a surgeon, a bachelor, a dedicated man . . .'

She leaned and rubbed noses with him. 'And here I am, being as bold as brass.' She pulled back. 'How long would we have gone on playing at being conspirators, always proper, always seeing each other only under pretexts, unless I had made the first move?'

Suddenly he relaxed and laughed. She smiled at him and ran a hand through his curly hair. He said, 'All right—child—I'm in love with you. Have you ever heard anything more grotesque than that?'

She came closer, her mouth seeking his. He felt for her waist, encircled it with arms like steel bands and didn't let her go until she moved her face under the pressure of his kiss. Then he released her and said, 'I'm going to take you straight home, and we're not going to see each other for a week, and in that length of time you'd better do a lot of serious thinking.'

He leaned to start the car. She laid a light hand upon his arm. 'Harry . . .? Will you do a lot of serious thinking too?'

'I promise us both to do that,' he said, almost grimly, started the car and turned to drive back up the lane. 'And all the while your uncle knew this—could happen?'

She snuggled close to him on the seat. 'I'll let you in on a little secret: I told my uncle I was in love with you two months ago.'

Harry drove up through the village and past The Gargoyle without looking round, then headed arrow-straight back through the countryside towards the distant city. He began going back in memory to some little things he'd noticed when he and Dr. Branch had been together; nothing obvious, just a look, a sidelong glance, a quiet thoughtfulness. And all the time he'd wondered if those things hadn't indicated that Dr. Branch suspected him of something altogether different.

He felt like a genuine fool.

Finally, nearing town, he laughed, shook his head, slid an arm round her waist and laughed again. She joined in. Perhaps she didn't precisely understand what was so ironically amusing to him, but then again, as he'd discovered quite vividly, she was a full woman, so on the other hand it was entirely possible that she *did* understand.

As they moved through the dusk-mottled streets she said, 'Don't bother to take me back to the hospital; just drive me home. Uncle Albert won't be expecting me to drive home with him anyway.'

CHAPTER ELEVEN

HIS EXCELLENCY

For Harry the period for self-recrimination passed after he'd seen Regina home. In the dark evening as he continued on to his flat he stopped fighting himself and let his imagination soar.

He couldn't deny he loved her; couldn't have denied that months before if he'd permitted himself to face it. As for visualising a future with her in it, the idea made him a little unsettled.

He put away the car, went up to his flat, considered a cold dinner, then remembered that he'd completely forgotten to offer Regina any tea or dinner. Perhaps it wasn't such a frightful oversight; if she felt as he felt, she couldn't have eaten anything anyway.

He showered, looked at himself in the mirror, then had an unsettling thought: What would Norman Belden think of Harry Blaydon at this moment? His reply to that came forcefully as he climbed into bed with a book. 'To hell with brother Belden!'

He went to sleep with a great sigh and awoke the following grey morning with a little start; he'd promised Dr. Haroush he'd be there to receive His Excellency Ibn Abdullah quite early.

There really was no great need for haste, he'd got up early enough, but all the same he made haste.

The streets were already stirring as he went down to the car, but there was still no sun, wouldn't be any sunlight for the matter of that for another couple of hours. It was a raw, cold, somewhat dismal morning with low dirty old clouds skimming along overhead not much higher than the rooftops.

Respite from this general gloom came when his thoughts turned to Regina as he drove through the nearly-empty streets. Additional respite was on ahead in the clean, lighted interior of Memorial Hospital.

George Laxalt was already there, which ordinarily was not the case; George's position as Chief Administrative Officer did not require him to be there to greet medical patients unless of course he chose to. He grinned at Dr. Blaydon and looked at his wrist.

'Evidently His Excellency broke the iron rule this morning and overslept.'

Harry could understand that. 'Look at that sky out there. I rather think His Excellency is accustomed to rising with the sun. In his country that's one thing they always have— sunshine.'

But they were both a little premature; His Excellency arrived moments later, preceded by a shining limousine full of what Harry took to be bodyguards. In the car following His Excellency's car came Dr. Saud Haroush, looking as though he hadn't been awake and dressed for very long.

George and Harry received His Excellency's personal emissary in the hospital foyer. He was an enormously dignified individual with a faintly antagonistic attitude.

The hostility was nothing Harry could quite put his finger on: it was in the emissary's sharp, cold eyes, in his militarily erect bearing, in his meticulous choice of words.

Then Dr. Haroush came forward, and immediately behind him Premier Ibn Abdullah himself, a man with the almond eyes of the Levant, the olive complexion, the hooked nose and, in his particular case, a sensuous, thick mouth. He was pleasant, shook hands, took the measure of both Harry Blaydon and George Laxalt, then asked if they wouldn't join him at coffee. As they steered His Excellency towards the restaurant the personal emissary and Dr. Haroush trailed along. So did three distinctly non-Arab gentlemen with coldly business-like faces and subdued clothing.

Harry began to warm to Ibn Abdullah, who, as the three of them took Dr. Branch's table in the restaurant said with a little smile, that it was so dark and dismal out he hadn't been sure his clock had been right when he rose.

'I miss the sunshine. But of course sunshine is helpful only to those who are young and healthy. I am certainly not the one, and, before you gentlemen are finished with me, it may turn out that I am not the other.'

Harry ordered coffee from a big-eyed waitress. It was about the time for the mob to arrive at the restaurant; he was conscious of that too. Without a doubt Dr. Belden would arrive shortly. Not Dr. Branch; he would come along later. When the coffee came His Excellency leaned on the table and said, 'Tell me, Dr. Blaydon; when you and Dr. Haroush spoke yesterday, what did you think?'

Harry wasn't quite sure what His Excellency meant. He said, 'What I thought of your condition, sir?'

'No. Of Dr. Haroush.'

That was easy to answer. 'Very well qualified, sir. An excellent physician. We wouldn't hesitate to have him on the staff here at Memorial.'

His Excellency seemed satisfied. He tasted the coffee, winked at George Laxalt and said, 'Too much water, eh? Well, when one is in Rome one wears a toga, eh?'

They all smiled.

Harry began to understand something about Ibn Abdullah; he kept his own counsel. He resembled the proverbial iceberg in that there was much more below the surface than there was above. His deliberate, almost courtly, movements might mistakenly be seen as an indication of great caution and uncertainty,

99

but Harry thought differently; His Excellency had a mind as sharp as a two-edged dagger. He gave that quiet-spoken, affable impression to disarm others. As an opponent, Harry thought he would be a very dangerous man. As an enemy he would be an undeviating executioner.

They finished their coffee, took the lift to the fourth floor, and there Harry introduced His Excellency to Norman Belden who had evidently chosen to skip morning coffee and wait for His Excellency on his own ground.

Norman said Dr. Branch had just arrived and would like His Excellency to come to his office for an official welcome to Memorial Hospital. Ibn Abdullah looked at Harry Blaydon with a kindly expression. 'I am interested, Doctor,' he murmured. 'Will you be the one who gives me the tests?'

Harry said, 'No, sir; I'm the one who will sit with Dr. Branch afterwards to judge the results.'

Ibn Abdullah was satisfied. 'Good. Then, when all that has been done, please come to see me.'

Harry promised to do that, watched the little party move away, led by Dr. Belden, and when George said, at his side, that the old gentleman seemed quite likeable, Harry smiled.

'As a friend I rather imagine you'd have a hard time finding anyone more likeable,
100

George. As an enemy . . .'

Harry shook his head.

Those two parted, each bound for his own office, and the physical acceptance of His Excellency, Ibn Abdullah, was over. The *official* welcoming process would now be inaugurated by Dr. Branch, probably with a tour of the building, an introduction to the skilled technicians who would make the examination and run the tests, and perhaps by a relaxed little talk in the Old Man's office.

Harry was in his office when one of the older nurses peeked in later, found him alone and said, 'Believe it or not, Dr. Blaydon, but he flirted with me seven years ago when he came over for his check-up!' She smiled and withdrew.

Harry lit his pipe, picked up the telephone and called Dr. Branch's house. The moment someone lifted the receiver he said, 'Good morning, sweetheart!'

Regina hung fire for a second then said, 'Suppose that had been the housekeeper, Harry? Or suppose Andrew had dropped round early?'

'I'd have excused myself and hung up, of course. But I knew it would be you!'

'How could you know that?'

'Masculine intuition,' he said, and chuckled.

Her voice sparkled with pleasure as she said, 'Sleep well last night?'

'Well; I realise this will come as a blow to

101

your ego, Queenie, but I slept like a log.'

'I didn't. And I resent the fact that you did. Is my uncle there?'

'Yes; but I haven't seen him yet because our illustrious patient arrived this morning at the crack of dawn—no—before the crack of dawn.'

'What's he like, Harry?'

'Not nearly as pretty as you are, nor as sweet, nor as wonderful to kiss. He's a likeable old man, quiet and philosophical, with a mind like a rapier beneath a façade of pleasant good-nature. But what I called about—how about dinner tonight?'

She said, 'I thought you'd never ask,' and laughed at him. 'I want to know what happens when you and my uncle have your correct little man-to-man talk.'

'Good. I'll be round to pick you up about six. Perhaps slightly later depending on things around here.'

She said, 'You mean you'll drive up to the front of the house very boldly; that we won't have to meet somewhere?'

'I'll be as bold as brass.'

' . . . As I was last night. Good-bye.'

'With my love, Regina.'

He'd scarcely replaced the telephone when Dr. Belden came in looking, for a change, as though there might be some hope for the world after all. He took a chair without waiting to be invited to do so, and said, 'He's a very remarkable person.' Of course Belden was speaking of Ibn Abdullah. 'He and Dr. Branch hit it off very well. Of course they've met before when His Excellency's come across for check-ups, but you'd have thought they were close friends.'

Harry, having been able to guess this was about as things would have gone in Dr. Branch's office, said, 'Did he mention any specific symptoms?'

Belden shook his head. 'You'd have thought it was simply a visit, a social call.'

Harry could also believe that. His personal appraisal of the Premier included the notion that Ibn Abdullah would be the very essence of stateliness and good manners even though he might privately be thinking along totally different lines from his host.

'We'll see that he's gone over thoroughly,' assured Norman. 'If you'd like you could supervise it all yourself, Harry.'

'No need. He'll be given just as thorough a series of tests without me—or you.'

Dr. Belden nodded. 'On the basis of eyes and general appearance, I'll hazard a loose guess. Not to be repeated of course.'

'Shoot,' Harry said, not too interested.

'Abdominal trouble of some kind.'

Harry grinned. 'You could have picked that up in the records, Norman.'

'No, not exactly. The records indicate more hypochondria than valid complaints. But I

103

think he really has something wrong with him. At least this time.'

Harry still wasn't too impressed. 'He's an old man. There's not an ambulatory human being past thirty, Norman, that doesn't have something wrong with him and you know it.'

Belden nodded, 'As you say. But I'm still betting on my hunch.' He rose, it was nearly noon. 'Care to join me for luncheon?'

'No thanks. I haven't even had time to go over the night-reports yet. His Excellency threw a small wrench into the works this morning.'

After Belden had departed Harry got busy with the paper-work that was always awaiting him every morning; George Laxalt got the same amount of paper-work on the management side, and the few, if any, top-echelon reports went to Dr. Branch for perusal. But the majority of medical reports, suggestions and memoranda, wound up on Harry Blaydon's desk.

He'd long since developed a sixth-sense; he could almost tell by looking at the signatures whether there was anything worth reading; of course he was more thorough than that, but this morning the only paper to hold his attention was one submitted by the third-floor consultant who said the African politico was well enough to return home.

To die, of course.

Harry made a small, solemn note of

approval and thought that if he had time that afternoon he'd go down and visit the old man. Death was a great leveller; a great, and sometimes the only, way men of totally different worlds could communicate.

He finished work at one o'clock. At one-thirty Emily popped in to say Dr. Branch would like to see Harry in his office, and to report that she'd been completely won over by Ibn Abdullah. With a grin Harry offered a warning.

'He's got you down for his harem, love. If you're not careful he'll steal you.'

She laughed, blushed and retreated.

Harry sat a moment organising his thoughts. He knew about how the forthcoming talk would go. First, they'd discuss His Excellency. Then they'd discuss something that made Harry redden a little as he thought of it—and smile.

Finally, he rose, pocketed his pipe, his pouch, and started to leave. His palms were as damp as the palms of a schoolboy about to face the parent of a schoolgirl!

CHAPTER TWELVE

AN UNSETTLING VISIT

Dr. Branch greeted Harry briskly, shooting him a quick look, then leaned over to straighten his desk. It was, in Harry's view, an excellent beginning since it meant the Old Man was just as uncertain as Harry was.

'His Excellency,' began Albert Branch, 'seems to me to have aged a good deal more than would be normal since his last visit, Harry.'

'He's charming, sir; we had coffee this morning.'

'Yes, I know. He told me.' Branch's grey eyes lifted and lingered on Harry. 'You made a good impression. He asked to have you in consultation. I told him you would be, in any case.'

'Anything definite on him yet?'

'Well, no, as a matter of fact he'll be going through the mill all the afternoon and perhaps tomorrow as well. But that personal man of his, Haroush ...' Dr. Branch leaned back in his chair. 'Nice chap. Very pleasant.'

Harry waited. Dr. Branch obviously had a reservation about Haroush. This interested Harry because he'd found nothing about the Middle-Easterner to make him wonder.

'Well qualified, Harry. I asked Emily to check up on him.'

In an attempt to expedite things Harry said, 'But you didn't approve of him.'

'Not personally, you understand. I just think he may be weak on diagnosis.'

Harry suddenly visualised Norman Belden leaning over and whispering to Dr. Branch. Harry said, 'Odd you should suspect something, Doctor. Norman Belden was in my office a while ago hinting at something seriously wrong with our patient.'

Dr. Branch made a little gesture. 'The tests will show, of course. But my personal feeling is that Haroush for some reason let his patient go a bit too long before bringing him to us.'

'That,' stated Harry, remembering something Haroush had said, 'wasn't exactly up to Dr. Haroush. I would imagine His Excellency has the same illusion our African politician had—that his country couldn't survive unless he were right there at the helm. For the African it has proved to be a tragic, and I should imagine unnecessary, sacrifice. For Ibn Abdullah the same may be true. In any case I wouldn't suggest anyone but His Excellency himself is at fault.'

'Maybe,' conceded Dr. Branch. 'Tea, Harry?'

'No, thank you.'

'If you don't mind I'll have a cup.' Dr. Branch punched a button, leaned towards the little grille on his desk and said, 'Could I have a cup of tea, Emily? Thank you.' He straightened up and looked at Harry. It was an uncomfortable look. 'Well, well; Queenie and I had a very pleasant little talk this morning.'

Harry said nothing. He had no inclination to help his mentor at all Dr. Branch smiled. 'I must tell you I'm very pleased, Harry.'

'Thank you, sir.'

'Yes. For a while there I thought it might be young Andrew Connell.'

Harry finally spoke up. 'It would doubtless be much better if it had been Andrew, sir.'

The Old Man's gaze widened a fraction. 'I understand. Queenie explained. You feel there is too great a difference in your ages. Well, let me tell you something. Emily in the outer office is fifty-five. I once considered asking her to marry me. I'm past seventy. Not much past, it is true, but still past, you see, and that's a damn lot more disparity, Harry, yet I faced it without a second thought.' Dr. Branch was warming to his subject. He leaned forward and said, 'Thirty-five, Harry, is *youth*.'

'If that is so, sir, what is twenty-one?'

'The same, Harry. Youth, of course. The point is, age can't ever be broken down in quite the way you're doing it. You know as well as I do that the difference between a man of sixty and one of seventy is slight. The difference between a man of twenty-five and one of thirty-five is slight. And you also are

108

aware that a woman of twenty-one is the equal of any woman of thirty-one. So where, will you please tell me, is all this great difference?'

Harry didn't answer. He didn't really have the chance. Dr. Branch's secretary came in with the Old Man's tea. She shot Harry a look, then withdrew without a word being spoken. Afterwards, the Old Man broke into Harry's organised words and took over the initiative.

'She will make a splendid wife, Harry, I've always felt the peril to doctors' marriages was that the average woman of lay stock wouldn't understand, nor be able to adjust to, sharing her husband night and day. But with Queenie—'

Harry laughed. Old Branch, interrupted, sat there gazing at him Harry said, 'You don't have to convince me, sir. I'm convinced. You had nothing to do with it. Regina would make the kind of wife a man could hope for and perhaps never encounter in a hundred years. I'm not at all unwilling to marry her. Of course, that hasn't actually come up yet, although I intend to see that it's mentioned very soon. And I'm not oblivious of the fact that having been brought up in your family she'd realise exactly what a medical man for a husband would be called upon to do, and what sacrifices she'd have to make.'

Dr. Branch lifted his cup, tasted the tea, set the cup down and said, 'I'm very pleased about this, Harry. I'm not very good at stating my emotions so you'll simply have to be satisfied with that.'

The telephone rang. Dr. Branch reached for it with a dry expression coming over his face. After he'd replaced the instrument he said, 'The college; I'm due over there this afternoon.' He looked at his hands on the desk a moment as though he might say something else, then reached for the teacup without speaking.

Harry went back to the topic under discussion before the telephone call. 'I'm glad we have your approval,' he said. 'I'm to take Regina out to dinner this evening?'

'Fine,' said Dr. Branch, then he scowled slightly. 'I anticipate an increase in my cost of living, Harry. The housekeeper does not live in, which means I'll either have to find one who will live in, or pay the present one enough to induce her to stay and get my dinner. I never could cook.'

Harry rose. 'Neither could I, and although I sympathise with your dilemma, sir, you must realise it will be difficult for me to shed any tears when I acquire a wife to cook for me, and you lose a niece.'

They smiled at one another. Harry left, smiled at Emily who was clearly interested in whatever they'd been discussing in there—she was, after all, Albert Branch's confidante of long standing—and strolled back to his own office.

A representative from the African leader called shortly before three o'clock to discuss procedures for withdrawing his employer from Memorial. Harry sent him down to see George Laxalt whose realm that was.

Andrew Connell called at three-thirty to enquire of Harry when the Board of Renewal would convene, and Harry also referred Andrew to Laxalt's office. He did this rather brusquely, so when the call was ultimately routed back to his line again, he wasn't surprised to hear Andrew say,

'I'm sorry we can't be friends, Doctor.'

Of course the answer was routine. 'We *can* be friends, Andrew. Professionally, probably ethically, and undoubtedly humanely—just not socially.'

'But you know perfectly well what I'm trying to do is right, Dr. Blaydon.'

'Right as rain,' Harry said. 'I'm sure that you and the Almighty have at least that much in common. If you'll excuse me . . .'

'Doctor, give me one reason for your attitude.'

Harry silently sighed, leaned back and said a little condescendingly, 'Andrew, my attitude in this as in a good many other things, is simply that hurling oneself at a problem like a blind bull is not the best way to solve things.'

'And you have a better way?'

'Much better.'

'Would you be good enough to explain it to

me?'

'I haven't the time just now. You'll have to excuse me.' Harry resolutely placed the telephone in its cradle and gazed at it as though expecting Andrew Connell to have devised some means for projecting himself bodily through it.

Half an hour later, when it was slightly past four in the afternoon, he completed the last of the paper-work, sauntered out to see what changes, if any, had been chalked up on the duty-roster outside Dr. Branch's office, then turned and started towards the lift. No changes had been made at all, which simply meant there was to be only routine surgery the ensuing day.

When he left the building it was beginning to spit with rain. The sky was darkening in all quarters, there were lights showing in houses and shops, even cars moving past had their lamps on. He made a gloomy appraisal of this night, which he'd wished to be more serene for his first official date with Regina Barkley Branch, then tramped towards his car.

There were a number of minor bills in his mail when he arrived at the flat, and he hadn't been home long enough to more than remove coat and tie, when Dr. Haroush appeared at his door, which was a distinct surprise.

Haroush said, 'Forgive me, Doctor. I got the address from your hospital registry. I have no business following you into your private life,

112

and I'm full of the most abject apologies . . .'

Harry had to smile at the anxious man's phraseology.

'Come in,' he said, holding the door for Haroush to enter. 'You need some brandy.' When Haroush looked as though he might protest, Harry held up a hand. 'Medicinal brandy, Doctor. I am aware men of your faith are opposed to liquor. It's raining out there and the possibility of pneumonia is quite good.'

He went to the kitchen, eyed his waiting dinner dryly, then returned to the sitting-room with two glasses. Dr. Haroush accepted his with thanks, peered in at the stuff and took the chair Harry indicated before sipping. He smiled. 'Very good, Dr. Blaydon. You certainly are qualified as a prescriptionologist.'

Harry laughed. The word was descriptive but hardly common. 'What can I do for you?' he asked, hoping that whatever it was wouldn't take long. He still had to bathe and dress and drive over to the Branch house.

Haroush's normally dusky cheeks were slightly pale, his black eyes were large. 'Doctor, this evening I saw the preliminary reports . . . some of them at any rate.'

Harry felt a little annoyed. No one was supposed to see those reports until they'd been checked, double-checked, then sent directly to the Chief or his assistant.

He said, 'Preliminaries don't mean very

113

much, Dr. Haroush.'

'Enough,' mumbled the other man. 'If a preliminary report says someone had better lose an arm, they will lose it.'

Harry's irritation moved up a notch. 'I don't understand the allegory,' he said, although that wasn't quite true; he understood it.

Dr. Haroush drained the last of his brandy. 'Doctor, the preliminaries indicate His Excellency may have a malignancy in the lower tract.'

Harry thought about this a moment. '*May* have,' he eventually said, 'is different from *has*. I can understand your concern, of course, but I'm a little surprised at your conclusion. There can be nothing positive until all tests are completed and judgements have been made. You know that.'

'Doctor, this isn't just any patient, nor am I someone else. Have you any idea what could happen to me if I miscalculated?'

Harry began to fathom the other man's dread. He looked into his brandy glass a moment, then said in a more humane tone of voice, 'Dr. Haroush, you told me yourself that His Excellency would not respond to your solicitations some time back. If he has an acute condition, how can he blame you now?'

'*He* won't.' said Haroush. 'But others will. Doctor, it's not simply a matter of losing a licence to practise medicine. Do you understand?'

114

Harry nodded and rose. 'Come to see me in the morning,' he said, led the other man to the door, patted his shoulder and said, 'The odds, Dr. Haroush, are all against a malignancy. Sleep on that. I'll look into things as soon as I can tomorrow.'

Haroush departed looking no more relieved than when he'd first arrived. Harry ran to shave and shower and dress. He would be late anyway but he wished to mitigate that fact as much as he could. He grimaced at himself in the bathroom mirror. Regina was going to get her first taste of what it would be like being married to him.

He also thought of Saud Haroush's dilemma. It seemed far-fetched to believe Haroush would be persecuted in the twentieth century because someone else might perish from a malignancy. Far-fetched and unreasonable. Of course the point was, not everyone was altogether in the twentieth century yet.

CHAPTER THIRTEEN

LOVE AND A STORMY NIGHT

Regina was waiting. She said her uncle had recently telephoned from the college to say he'd be a bit late, so he would have his dinner at a restaurant.

As they left the house a streaked moon jumped out through some dark clouds and an occasional star shone. The smell of rain was strong, and lights were reflected upon and against pavement, walls, even the sky above.

'Beautiful night,' she said, smiling at him as they got into the car.

He thought she was being facetious and said, 'Ideal. An ideal night for haunting house. Did you remember to bring along your broom?'

He took her to a quiet, expensive restaurant specialising in roast beef, and ordered drinks while they waited for the meal to be served. He told her of Haroush's unexpected visit and when she looked worried he shrugged it off.

'I think he may be a little too imaginative. But even if what he says is true, and granting even the improbability of Ibn Abdullah's physical disturbance turning out to be something fatal—Haroush can simply stay in this country, or emigrate to some other country where his skills would be appreciated. I'm not even sure that in Trans-Arabia they'd go as far as he implied.'

She wanted to know all about the illustrious patient himself. She said he was always in the newspaper. He told her what he'd seen and heard, and also what he'd surmised. During the conversation their dinners arrived. While they ate she said, 'Andrew made one of his

116

tiresome calls an hour or so before you arrived. He said he'd spoken to you today and you'd said you knew a way to keep Uncle Albert out of the operating theatre.'

Harry grimaced. 'Andrew is like some kind of evil spirit; he floats into one's awareness when he has no business there at all. I simply told him one didn't have to be as rude in one's efforts as he was, and I also said I didn't have the time to explain it to him. Frankly, I wish he'd just go along tending to his knitting—or pill-pushing, rather.'

She smiled. 'Are you annoyed?'

He looked up and smiled. 'Hardly. It would be very difficult under the present conditions.'

She said, 'We've polished off His Excellency and poor Andrew. Now tell me about Uncle Albert and the college.'

He actually knew very little so it ended up with her telling him that Dr. Branch was gradually becoming quite interested. She knew that, as she said, because her uncle was an open book to her. He of course related what had been said in the Old Man's office that day, then he said, 'And we discussed—us.'

She nodded. 'I was leading up to that, of course. He was pleased, wasn't he?'

Harry nodded, watching soft light touch her face and throat. 'He was pleased. In fact he . . .'

She sat waiting. 'Yes . . . ?'

'Will you marry me, Regina?'

She paused a moment before nodding very softly towards him. 'If you're sure that's what you want, Harry.'

'I'm sure.'

To alleviate the sensation of prickly discomfort rising from this very intimate conversation he told her of Dr. Branch's very practical approach to such a union. He also told her he wholeheartedly concurred.

'You see, I was late for our date tonight. It was through no wish on my part at all, Queenie. What I'm saying—'

'I know what you're saying,' she smiled. 'Uncle Albert and I talked for a solid hour last night before the fire, about the duties, obligations, responsibilities of men such as you and he. Harry; I'll keep your dinner warm, make excuses for your tardiness to our friends, and try very hard never to feel that you love your trade more than you love me. That's what my uncle told me I'd have to do.' She reached over on a sudden impulse and patted his hand across the dining-table. 'He also said that under the new arrangement, with you acting for him as Chief Consultant at Memorial, I might even have to settle for seeing less of you, now.'

He waited for her to finish then said, 'I think your uncle was correct. When he said surgeons should be celibates, I'm beginning to think he was right.'

She shook her head. 'I'm not. Anyway how

118

does one regulate love? Can you turn it on and off like a water tap? I can't.'

He couldn't either.

They left the restaurant to go to stand in the dismal, wet gloom for a moment beside the car. She said it was as though the world were being purged of all evil. He cast a sidelong glance at her. 'You have a poetic soul.'

They drove slowly back towards her home. When they reached the home she said, 'Our conspiring took an odd turn, Harry.'

'A *better* turn, love.' He reached, and she came willingly into his arms. She whispered that his shaving lotion smelled wonderful. He kissed her, felt her burrowing closer and kissed her again.

The lamp outside the front door burst into glaring light. They moved apart just as Dr. Branch peered out into the stormy darkness. Regina sighed and said Harry ought to come in for a moment. He felt about as she did; he'd much rather remain in the darkened car with her.

They got out, strolled hand-in-hand up to the door and on into the hall where Dr. Branch in an old-fashioned smoking jacket and slippers, welcomed them with a big smile.

'That's how people contract pneumonia,' he boomed, and herded them into the sitting-room where a delightful fire glowed redly on the hearth. 'Well, Harry, I do believe I'm launched upon the world as a lecturer.

119

Evidently word has spread that I'll be holding seminars at the college and Emily telephoned a while back to say one of the great newspaper chains called this afternoon to enquire whether I'd be interested in writing a syndicated column or not. And there was another call for lectures.'

Regina, removing hat and coat, said she'd go and make some tea. Harry went to a chair, sat down, crossed his legs and groped through his pockets for his pipe. It began to look as though all the Old Man had needed, actually, had been a slight shove in the right direction. He lit up while Dr. Branch took a nearby chair and the pair of them sat silently watching the fire for a moment.

Outside, a gust of wind rattled windows and whooped away over the rooftops. A car made its careful way through the night, lamps glaring, wheels swishing on the wet road.

The Old Man suddenly leaned forward. 'Well . . ?' he whispered, looking vitally interested.

Harry smiled. 'She agreed.'

'Ahh, fine. Wonderful, my boy. Congratulations. But when?'

They hadn't got round to setting a date for the wedding. Harry simply said, 'Soon, I hope.'

The Old Man leaned back in his chair, a slight smile around his lips, both hands resting on the arms of the chair while he relaxedly sat gazing into the fire. Harry was not insensitive to what was probably passing through his chief's mind. In a different manner the same thoughts held him silent and relaxed. He was at peace, and the wild night beyond the windows only heightened that sense of serenity.

When Regina returned with the tea-tray she glanced at them and said, 'Am I keeping you up, by any chance?'

Harry laughed. 'Far from it.'

She served them, then took an occasional chair slightly to one side and sat down. She could see them both but her eyes lingered longest on Harry's profile. 'What do men talk about in these circumstances?' she asked, goading one or the other of them into conversation.

Her uncle smiled gently, 'It's not what they talk of, child, it's what they think.'

'All right; what do they *think* of, then?'

Harry said, 'You—and the future. What do women think of?'

'The same thing. You and the future.'

'Rapport,' grinned Harry. 'A good way to start out.'

Dr. Branch avoided this somewhat devious means of communication and asked a direct question. 'When do you suppose would be a good time for a marriage, Queenie?'

She was drinking tea and made no effort to reply until she'd finished. 'Whenever my lord and master desires, Uncle Albert.'

They all smiled and Harry said, 'What's wrong with tonight?' He then rose, put his cup aside and said it was getting late; that both he and Dr. Branch had better get their rest because they'd be called upon to assess the results of Ibn Abdullah's tests the next day. He and the Old Man shook hands then Regina went to the door with him.

They kissed tenderly. He said, 'Your uncle brought up a good point. When?'

She smiled into his eyes. 'I mean what I said. Whenever you want.'

He held her very close. She was warm and supple.

'I want,' he whispered, 'I want you very much.'

She touched his face with a cool palm. 'I know, my love. It is a mutual feeling, in case your training didn't include a course on emotionalism in women—they feel the same needs as men.'

'Think about it,' he said, releasing her. 'I'll ring you in the morning.'

They kissed again, lingeringly this time, then he left the house, bowed into the wind all the way to his car, and headed for home, his emotions just about as tumultuous as the night through which he drove.

There was scarcely any traffic, which was understandable; people would never need a very good reason to be abroad on such a night, and yet the rain which had fallen earlier seemed to have dwindled off until only now and again did little stinging drops slash earthward from the harassed heavens.

When Harry reached his flat there was a note pushed under the door. It had evidently arrived by special delivery since it was neither stamped nor franked. He took it to the kitchen with him while he got a glass of water and read it while leaning upon the sink.

A doctor named Geoffrey Saul had telephoned Memorial from Kenya that his patient had died shortly after landing there. Geoffrey Saul was the personal physician of that African politician who'd only just recently been discharged from Memorial.

Harry took the note back to the sitting-room with him and stood by a window gazing out. It hadn't been necessary for someone to go to all that trouble to let him know. He'd probably have read about it in the newspapers, or perhaps the next day at his office he'd have heard of the man's passing.

Sometimes people needed to feel that someone really cared. Harry, feeling slightly depressed, since he'd had several talks with the dying man and had liked him, pocketed the note and went to take a shower before retiring.

He began wondering what Ibn Abdullah's fate would be. He also recalled Dr. Belden's cold-blooded observation that it would be better if the African didn't die at Memorial.

Well, Belden would be pleased to learn the

old man had had the decency to wait until he got back to his own continent, at least, before passing on.

As for Ibn Abdullah, Harry began to have an uncomfortable feeling. It wasn't what Dr. Haroush had said, nor what he'd implied, it was just that Harry was tired. He told himself that as he climbed into bed; tired and unduly aroused over all that had happened this night.

Finally, of course, there was that pathetic note in his coat pocket.

He should have been more immune to death; he'd been facing it all his mature life. As a matter of fact he was immune to it—but only to the extent that he recognised its urgency and its inexplicable necessity, when it touched someone with whom he'd only had casual contact. But at Memorial Hospital where he was in a position to know most of the people he worked upon, it was different. A man would have had to possess a heart of stone not to feel depressed when someone died.

He closed his eyes, forced his thoughts into more pleasant channels, reflected briefly on how unexpectedly well his scheme to divert Albert Branch into the lecture field had worked, and fell asleep thinking of Regina; of the way she wrinkled her nose when she smiled, of how easily she blushed, of how solidly practical she could be when the occasion arose, and finally, how wonderfully warm and soft and yielding she was in his arms.

As he slept the wild night tore clouds apart, revealed a high, white moon, and off on a far-distant horizon where the clouds were congregating to assault some other place, there was an ominous blackness.

By morning it would all have passed.

CHAPTER FOURTEEN

UNPLEASANT NEWS

Harry hadn't a chance to go to Dr. Branch's office until nearly noon. An unexpected rash of routine matters lying somewhere between his responsibility and the realm of George Laxalt arose to keep him occupied in his office.

He rang Regina because he'd promised. They talked for some time—until a nurse came to say a gentleman caller was waiting outside—then he promised to call in that night and rang off.

As soon as he recognised his visitor he wished he'd had enough presence of mind to ask the nurse his name first. It was Andrew Connell. Harry perfunctorily nodded, pointed to a chair, and lit his pipe. He meant this visit to he brief. He also thought he knew what had impelled the younger man to come to see him. Without any preliminaries Harry said, 'You may or may not have heard, Andrew, that Dr. Branch is engaged to present a series of lectures at the College of Surgeons. He has also been asked to give other lectures, and there has been some interest shown by a major newspaper network respecting a syndicated column. Now if you don't think these sidelines will keep him occupied, you are mistaken. And if you're wondering if these were part of what I meant when I said there were other ways to ease him out of the operating theatre, I can tell you that they are. Although I'll also have to confess that I actually had very little to do with them.'

Andrew sat through this somewhat lengthy and pedantic harangue, then said, 'I see. But of course he may still perform operations.'

Harry leaned forward a little. 'He can also breathe, Andrew, and eat, and walk, and think.'

Andrew stiffened. 'Doctor; I'm sorry that I've angered you. My point, quite simply, concerns Dr. Branch's continued practice of surgery. That's all.'

'And I've just explained to you that he is being weaned away from it; that perhaps within six months or a year he'll simply not have the time.'

'Ahhh; but that doesn't cover the inclination, does it? Dr. Blaydon, I know

Albert Branch very well. Surgery is his life.'
Andrew gave a disagreeable smile. 'Your way
is very thoughtful and considerate, but it is
sidestepping the primary issue—which is
simply that he *must not perform surgery any
longer!*'

Harry sat and studied the younger man for a
while. There was no point in continuing this
conversation. Harry had his own convictions,
Andrew Connell had his convictions. Then
Andrew said, 'I framed a letter to the Board of
Renewal, Doctor. I haven't sent it off yet. I was
ready to when I encountered another
physician who feels as I do.'

Suddenly Harry was alert. 'Another
physician, Andrew? He wouldn't by any
chance be here at Memorial?'

'No, he's not here. But he told me he knew
of a man who was working here who also felt
as he and I feel. I'm to take my letter to that
man tonight. If he likes it he'll add one of his
own.'

'Very melodramatic,' murmured Harry,
affecting a slight scorn he didn't altogether
feel. Actually, he was beginning to suspect
what was in the offing; the one thing he wished
at all hazards to prevent; a meeting between
Andrew Connell and Norman Belden. 'Who is
the person employed here at Memorial?'

Andrew stood up. 'I won't know until I
meet him. Doctor, I'm most certainly not out
to persecute the only man who has ever

127

genuinely helped me. I want you to believe that. I'd also like it if you understood that I want to save him from himself as much as you and Regina do. But I cannot in good conscience accept your long drawn-out way of accomplishing it. You know as well as I do that any day now someone will he brought in for an operation here at Memorial and *he'll* be in charge. What will follow is murder pure and simple—with you as an accessory.'

Harry's usually even temper was heating up towards the gangling young man across the desk. He said, 'Listen, Andrew; the delusion of godliness among medical men is second only in infamy—at least in my eyes—to the majority greed for quick, large fees, from people who can be bilked. You are standing here guilty of the first; I wonder if, as the years pass, you won't also succumb to the latter.' Harry stood up. 'I can assure you that from this very moment, I am in effect Chief Consultant Surgeon of Memorial.'

'Officially, Dr. Blaydon?'

'Not officially. Officially I'm Acting Chief Consultant.'

'Then Dr. Branch can still walk in and take over.'

Harry said, 'You don't know much about surgical techniques, obviously.' No one can *walk in* and take over. At Memorial we have briefings; we co-ordinate all knowledge and the techniques to be used. *Then* we march in,

128

as you say. If Dr. Branch or anyone else hadn't been present at a briefing, believe me, he could not participate. He could observe—but then so can you. But neither he nor you could participate.'

Andrew frowned a little. 'Are you telling me that from today on, Dr. Blaydon, Albert Branch will no longer be operating at Memorial?'

Harry hadn't explicitly implied that but he'd most certainly hinted at it. So he said, 'I'm convinced that very shortly that will be the case, and from now on, it's my intention to keep him occupied in other fields so that he won't have time for briefings.'

Andrew seemed to waver. Finally, moving towards the door he said, 'Doctor, the Board won't convene for a couple more weeks, will it? I wonder if you'd feel like giving me your word that you'll have Dr. Branch out of the surgical field by that time?'

Harry teetered on the brink of a direct answer. The reason he finally demurred was that he felt no compulsion to comply. He said, 'Let's just leave it this way, Andrew. You call me a couple of days before the Board convenes, and by that time I'll either have him out of active surgical undertakings, or you can appear before the Board with your demand to that effect.'

Andrew nodded. It was a compromise as far as he was concerned, but one only had to look at Harry Blaydon's square jaw and implacable eyes to realise that was the best Andrew was going to get out of him.

After Andrew had departed Harry dropped into his chair. He had no idea who that other physician was who'd promised to introduce Andrew to Dr. Belden; probably someone who knew Albert Branch by reputation only, but whose zeal—and probably jealousy—rendered him amenable to tearing down Dr. Branch.

But honestly, Andrew and the other man, whatever their private motives, were correct. The Old Man was not fit to perform operations any longer.

His telephone rang. It was George Laxalt calling to ask whether Harry had conferred yet with the Old Man on Ibn Abdullah's condition. Harry said that he had not and asked why George wanted to know. The answer was cryptic.

'Newsmen, Harry. There are three in my outer office at the moment, and the telephone has been ringing constantly. We'll have to put out some kind of statement today.'

Harry promised to call back when he knew anything, then rang off, rose and left the office. He met Dr. Belden in the hall; Belden also wanted to know the results of His Excellency's tests. Harry had to reiterate what he'd just told Laxalt. Belden nodded, then said, 'His Excellency's man Haroush is moping about the place as if the worst was about to happen.'

Harry strolled up to Dr. Branch's office, asked Emily about the note he'd found under his door the night before and was told it had been personally delivered by one of the consulate members on orders of the dying man shortly before he actually died.

She said, 'Dr. Branch was also to be given one, but I sidetracked his note until this morning. I just didn't want him disturbed last night.'

Harry nodded, asked if the Old Man were in, and was told to go on through the door, that Dr. Branch was available.

As soon as he entered the inner office and saw Dr. Branch's face he knew something was wrong. The Old Man said, 'Good morning,' in a grave tone, and pointed to a chair beside the desk. 'Haroush was correct.' He handed Harry some papers. There remained a number of cloudy X-ray exposures on the desk. Dr. Branch sat studying them morosely.

The tests were actually co-ordinated clues leading towards a rather obvious conclusion. Carcinoma. Harry re-read them, particularly the ones indicating a stomach disturbance. When he finished he asked if the earlier reports had been incorporated. Dr. Branch had the answer to that.

'No need; I went down there and looked at them an hour ago. It really was a duodenal ulcer when it was so diagnosed.'

Harry felt a tiny measure of relief. 'Then how long has this present condition existed?'

Dr. Branch threw up his hands. 'The hell of it is that asking questions of someone with an ulcer is that they define one stomach pain pretty much as like all other intestinal discomforts. The X-rays aren't too clear.' The Old Man leaned upon his desk. 'Explorative, Harry,' he said sombrely. 'I'm afraid that's about it. But take the reports back with you and study them. Maybe you can come up with something less . . . involved.'

Fatal was what he'd almost said.

Harry nodded, reached for the X-ray exposures and sat back again. 'Too bad about the old African, sir.'

'Yes. I don't like starting a day with news like that. Have you been down to speak to Ibn Abdullah yet?'

Harry shook his head. He'd meant to, and he was aware that he'd promised His Excellency to drop in, but it hadn't been feasible. As he rose he said, 'I'll do it today,' and went to the door.

'Harry,' the Old Man said quietly. 'I've got to go over to the college this afternoon. Suppose you drop in at my house tonight and we can discuss the case there.'

Harry nodded and walked out. He'd promised to drop in at the house anyway, only not with the intention of sitting around talking shop.

132

After returning to his office he went over the results of the many tests His Excellency the Premier of Trans-Arabia had been subjected to. The one bright note in that forest of cryptic writing was the statement that the man's heart was as strong as the heart of a bull. People likely to have to undergo surgery need, above everything else, good hearts.

In most other ways as well His Excellency was in fair shape, considering his age. In fact one report indicated that his lungs were as clear as those of a young man.

But the tests on His Excellency's lower body were less hopeful. There was no actual way of telling from the outside just exactly how extensive the cancer was, of course, and since the man'd been bothered by stomach pains for a number of years, even trying to pinpoint the beginning of the carcinoma from that standpoint was too uncertain to be relied upon.

Harry did not favour exploratory surgery as a general rule. On the other hand, as Dr. Branch had suggested, in this case there seemed to be no alternative to it.

He rang up Norman Belden and asked him to call in at the office. Then he filled a pipe, lit up and sat in thoughtful silence until Belden arrived. Wordlessly, he handed the reports to Belden, leaned back and smoked while the other surgeon read, then more slowly and thoroughly, re-read.

Finally, Belden put the sheaf of papers aside and picked up the X-ray exposures. After a moment he put them aside and raised his eyes looking annoyed.

'Well . . . ?' he asked. 'Has Dr. Branch given his opinion?'

Harry nodded. 'Yes. Mine is the same. I'm waiting now to hear whether you concur.'

Norman looked at the murky exposures on the desk.

'Explorative surgery?'

Harry inclined his head again. 'That's it, I'm afraid.' He rose and put aside his pipe. 'I'll go to prepare him. Norman, George's been bothered by newsmen.'

Belden understood. 'They won't get a word out of me,' he said, and walked out of the office behind Harry Blaydon.

It was past noon. Harry hadn't eaten, but at the moment he didn't feel very much like it anyway. He strolled the almost empty corridors to the wing where distinguished patients were billeted, nodded to the neat, powerfully-built man sitting outside a particular door reading, and asked if His Excellency was alone. The guard said that he was; that Dr. Haroush had left some five or ten minutes earlier and no one else had entered His Excellency's room since. Harry thanked the man, squared his shoulders and walked in.

CHAPTER FIFTEEN

CARCINOMA!

It is a fact, and doctors learn it earlier than most people, that the world's great men lying in a hospital bed, never look great at all. They usually don't even look average.

Except for his carefully trimmed salt-and-pepper beard, almond-shaped black eyes, and bushy greying mane, the Premier of Trans-Arabia might have been some pedlar off the streets of a large city.

Of course there was the room; very airy, with double windows, thick carpeting, a television set and a short-wave transceiver on a steel table, plus some elegant non-hospital furniture. But His Excellency in the white hospital bed looked small and thin and old as Harry Blaydon walked silently over, smiling, and His Excellency said in a soft, quiet voice, 'Well, well. Are you the Angel of Darkness or the spirit of hope?' His black eyes warmed a little.

Harry drew up a chair and felt the patient's wrist. The pulse was good, neither fast nor sluggish. He said, studying the lined, strong old face, 'It may depend entirely upon your viewpoint, Your Excellency, but as a rule doctors like to imagine themselves as spirits of hope.'

Ibn Abdullah was evidently a dyed-in-the-wool fatalist.

He said, 'So be it, Doctor. You may view yourself as the spirit of hope. But, tell me how much hope there is, and in what degree, I am allowed to believe.'

'Your Excellency, you will require abdominal surgery.'

The old eyes probed a moment, then the Arab's voice turned very soft as he said, 'So you see, Spirit of Hope, no one lives one stroke of the heart beyond his time, does he?'

Harry put the old man's limp hand across his chest.

'There is no reason to believe that your allotted time has expired.'

'But surgery . . .'

'Your Excellency, you could require surgery for almost anything.'

'Doctor!' The dark eyes flashed dull fire. Then the look was gone. 'Please, what are the facts?'

'A disturbance in your stomach which may turn out to be serious.'

'May? Is that all you can tell me?'

'At present, yes. That's why you will require surgery. So that we can determine the seriousness.'

Ibn Abdullah looked away for a moment then back again. 'Cancer . . . ?'

Harry permitted the last echo of that

whispered, dread word to die completely before he said. 'Very probably, Your Excellency. That's why those technicians kept trying to determine when you first noticed symptoms.'

'But how could I tell them? You know very well I've always had a stomach ailment.'

'Yes. So now we operate to determine the degree of seriousness.'

They were back where they'd started. Harry was no longer smiling and His Excellency, attempting to rally from what had to be a stunning body-blow, gazed unseeingly out of a window where winter sunshine brightened damp buildings and coaxed a smile from what few shrubs and trees hadn't been denuded by the wind.

His Excellency looked at Harry and smiled. 'Haroush kept telling me to come here.'

Harry felt relieved. 'Haroush is a very good physician.'

The old Arab's lips parted. 'Of course it won't look at all good for him if I die.'

'You could mitigate that by simply writing the facts on a slip of paper.'

Ibn Abdullah squinted. 'Of course. Well, I'll take care of Dr. Haroush. He won't suffer in any case.'

'There is me other thing, Your Excellency: The Press. They are here now insisting on some kind of statement.'

'Well, Dr. Blaydon, isn't that your

department?'

'No, sir, not entirely. Your condition is your own business. Memorial will protect your right to privacy.'

'I see. Very noble.' Ibn Abdullah smiled up at Harry as the latter rose to stand gazing down at the frail old man in the bed. 'In that case lie to them, Doctor. It will never do for anyone to let my countrymen know I am dying.'

'You're not dying,' contradicted Harry, feeling a little distress.

Ibn Abdullah shrugged. 'All right. Tell them that. Tell them it's the old ulcer again and that I'll be up and out of here in a week or two. Tell them, that for a man my age I am in remarkably excellent health.'

'That happens to be the truth,' grinned Harry. 'Your heart is as strong as a bull's heart, your lungs are absolutely clear.'

How nice,' murmured the old Arab. 'It's only my stomach that is going to kill me. All right, Doctor, all right; I'm overstating the case. Tell me now—when will I go under the knife?'

Harry and Dr. Branch hadn't discussed that. All he could say was, 'Soon, sir. I'll be back and let you know.'

After he'd escaped Harry stopped in the hall to light his pipe. The burly man put aside that newspaper he'd been reading, thoughtfully studied Harry, then said, 'Doctor,

138

off the record, how is he?'

'Surprisingly sound for an old man.' Harry smiled and paced slowly back to his own office. He'd scarcely started framing the non-committal press release to be taken to George Laxalt, when Norman Belden came in, took a chair and said, 'Where in hell is the Old Man? I was in his office just now and Emily said he'd be gone the rest of the day.'

Harry said, 'At the college, I suppose. At least that's where he told me he had to go today. Why, what's come up?'

'Well. Nothing exactly, Harry, except that I wanted to discuss the Premier's case with him.' Belden's sharp features darkened. 'How does he expect to run this place and the college simultaneously?'

Harry smiled. 'Norman, last week you were in here beating your head against the wall because you didn't think the Old Man should even be here.'

Belden didn't dispute that, but he said, 'I'm perfectly willing to confer with you, Harry. But don't you think it'd be better for morale all round if the Old Man would announce that he won't be available and that problems hereafter should be routed through you?'

Harry puffed and studied Dr. Belden a moment then said, 'I think it's an excellent idea. I'll take it up with him when we meet this evening. Anything else?'

Belden looked at the large yellow tablet

139

Harry had been writing upon when he walked in. 'Nothing important,' he said, rose and went to the door. There, he turned and said, 'Haroush wants to see you.'

Harry was resigned. 'Send him along.'

After Belden's departure he went back to picking bland words for the report on the health of His Excellency, the Premier of Trans-Arabia. It wasn't difficult but one had to be especially cautious in the choice of words. By the time Saud Haroush knocked timidly, then entered, Harry had the thing finished. He greeted his visitor with a genial wave towards a chair and handed him the paper.

'How will that translate?' he asked.

Dr. Haroush read, pursed his lips, squinted his eyes, scratched the tip of his somewhat prominent nose, then broke into a broad smile. 'Very well. It will come out to mean that His Excellency has a very minor abdominal occlusion and will shortly be relieved of it and be able to return home.'

Harry accepted the paper and looked dubiously at it. He hadn't meant the news release to be *that* bland. One glance at Haroush's expression of enormous relief, however, and Harry decided to let it stand.

He looked at his watch and said, 'Would you care to join me at luncheon, Doctor?'

Haroush was surprised. 'At two in the afternoon?'

Harry grinned all the way to the door. 'In
140

general practice one can regulate one's habits. In a place like Memorial Hospital, Doctor, one is lucky if lunch can be arranged by two o'clock.'

Not until they were going down to the lower floor and were alone inside the lift did Harry tell his companion exactly what the decision was: 'Explorative surgery to determine what progression has ensued since His Excellency has had the growth.'

Haroush crumpled up. 'He will die, of course, and for me, it will be the same thing.'

Harry explained 'I've already explained it all to His Excellency. He said that if he'd listened to you in the first place the growth wouldn't be as large as it may now be. He said he'd exonerate you in writing from any blame whatsoever.'

Haroush wasn't placated. 'Of course, Doctor, of course; he is a magnanimous person. But who in my country would ever believe he'd written such a thing? All that will matter is that he is dead, and that I was his personal physician.

By the time the lift stopped, Dr. Haroush had control of himself again. He marched beside Harry into the nearly deserted dining-room, pale and stricken-looking, but with a firm step.

He would, however, have nothing to eat, asking only for a cup of strong black coffee. Harry ordered the prepared luncheon then

141

said, 'Look, Doctor, he isn't dead. There is an even chance he won't be dead for a long while yet.'

'You said that last night. You said the odds favoured no malignancy. What do you say today, Dr. Blaydon?'

Harry sighed; he would have expected to be blamed for something he had absolutely no control over, nor knowledge of, by laymen, but when it came from another man of medicine who have must have also been blamed many times, it was a little different.

'Today I say, Dr. Haroush, you must get hold of yourself. When we schedule surgery you will want to observe. I'll see that full arrangements are made. But in the meanwhile, why don't you try and think back to the time when His Excellency might have first noticed something other was wrong besides that damned duodenal ulcer. That might help. Not much, perhaps, but a little.'

Mainly, Harry wanted Haroush occupied. It was a kind of therapy all in itself, keeping overwrought people busy. It rather annoyed him to think he'd have to use this stratagem against a fellow practitioner, but on the other hand Saud Haroush was by temperament different from the Blaydons, Beldens and Branches of this world.

The luncheon came and Harry started to eat at once because he was starved, and once when he glanced up, he saw Haroush looking into his coffee cup as though expecting some divine message to emerge there.

What Dr. Haroush needed was a stiff drink, but barring medicinal alcohol, which wasn't bottled with drinking in mind, there wasn't very much in the way of whisky or scotch around the place.

They returned to Harry's office. By that time Haroush was either becoming numb with fatalistic resignation, or was struggling to bolster up some kind of defensive system inside himself; in either case he looked less pale and agitated as he said, 'You are very kind. I saw that in your eyes when we first met. His Excellency said he would trust your judgement in anything pertaining to your profession. Of course I will do the same. But if His Excellency must die, then I think I'd better just stay in this country.'

Harry said, 'Suit yourself, Doctor. I'll do whatever I can to help you. However, even if the growth is inoperable, you know that His Excellency may still live another six month or a year.'

'Surgery will set the thing to growing throughout his body like wildfire,' groaned Haroush.

Harry couldn't argue that point; it was an acknowledged fact that surgery did, in fact, stimulate cancers. In fact there just wasn't much more Harry could say at all.

It was getting on for four in the afternoon.

He got rid of Dr. Haroush very diplomatically and gently, hastened along to Laxalt's office with the press-release, and stood by while George read it with a worried face, then heaved a big sigh and said it was quite good.

'Says just enough and not one thing more. That's the way they should be written. I'll pass it out as soon as my secretary's had a chance to make copies. Thanks, Harry. Anything else?'

'I'm on my way home.'

Laxalt looked at his wrist, then nodded. 'It's been a fast-moving day,' he said. 'All right; if anything comes up I'll call you at home.'

'Later on I'll be with Dr. Branch at his house.'

Laxalt nodded over that as well.

Harry went back to his office, slipped into his overcoat and headed for the lift. What was bothering him now was exactly what had been bothering Andrew Connell and Norman Belden for a long time. With anyone as important as the Premier of Trans-Arabia, Albert Branch would unquestionably scrub up with the surgical team as its chief!

CHAPTER SIXTEEN

BRIEF MOMENTS ALONE

He bathed and changed at home then drove directly to the Branch house, not out of any sense of urgency to confer with Dr. Branch, but because he wanted a few minutes alone with Regina before her uncle got home from the college. It was good thinking. By the time he knocked on the Branch front door it was not quite six-thirty; there was reason enough to believe the Old Man wouldn't show up for another half hour at the least.

Regina met him in a housedress and apron. She looked surprised. 'You weren't due for a while yet,' she said, and closed the door behind him.

He smiled. 'Had to get here early to steal a kiss.'

She threw both arms around his shoulders, strained upwards and met his lips with a warm, firm mouth. She hugged him very hard, then stepped back. He said that was much better and permitted her to lead him into the kitchen where, she explained, since it was the housekeeper's day off, she'd been preparing her uncle's supper. She said she'd set an extra place.

He protested. 'But we were going out to

dinner.'

Her answer was practical. 'I know. But couldn't I induce you to try my cooking just this once?'

'Sweetheart, it's too much bother.'

She looked up, smiling. 'It's not any bother for a woman to prepare meals for men she loves. If you insist, I'll prepare Uncle Albert's dinner, then pop it into the oven to keep warm, but that dries out the food. It also leaves him to eat alone, which to me has always been synonymous with punishment.'

'I'll stay,' he said. 'Can I help?'

She nodded. 'Just sit on that stool over there and tell me everything that happened today.'

He obeyed, perched on the stool, related to her most of what had occurred, neglecting to mention Andrew, and ended up watching the easy, perfectly co-ordinated way she moved.

She was interested in the Premier. She asked what his chances were and of course Harry could only say what he'd been telling others all day: 'There's no sure way to guess, love.'

She turned. 'You will do an exploratory, Harry?'

He nodded. 'Probably schedule it for the next day or two.'

'And—Uncle Albert will perform the actual operation?'

They exchanged a long glance and he said nothing. He knew what she was thinking; he'd noticed the increasing puffiness due to inflammation of the joints in her uncle's hands too.

She said, 'We didn't quite succeed after all, did we?'

He thought about that a moment, then told her of Andrew's threat. She wiped her hands at the sink and said, 'Will Dr. Belden team up with Andrew?'

He was sure of that. 'Very probably he will, yes. I suppose I could have circumvented their meeting, Queenie, but I didn't for the simple reason that what could have been prevented tonight, would eventually have happened anyway.'

She went to the stove, worked a moment then said,

'Harry? Can you keep him from performing that operation?'

He'd wondered about that himself, while he'd been hastily changing clothes at his flat. There were ways, of course, but they weren't very diplomatic; they weren't even very honest. 'I suppose so,' he muttered.

She turned. 'Then you must do it, musn't you?'

He regarded her soberly and said, 'It will depend on what he has in mind. I was to see him tonight, get his ideas.'

She understood. 'And when he's told you, then you can devise some way, can't you?'

That had been his idea but as he now said, it

147

was treachery pure and simple. She came over and put a hand upon him, saying that he was now having the same pains she'd had when he'd accused her of misplaced loyalty that first time they'd talked.

It was true, of course; that was precisely what was bothering him. He finally stood up, took her hands in his and drew her closer. 'I'll see to it,' he murmured, then kissed her, felt the length of her body loosen against him, and had two distinct sensations, one of distaste for himself, the other of desire for her.

He released her to go and see to whatever it was she was cooking on the stove, lit his pipe absent-mindedly and sat down again on his stool.

To clear the air he said, 'Have you given any thought to the wedding?'

She shot him a dazzling smile. 'I haven't given any thought to anything else. The housekeeper thinks it should be postponed until June because she says that's the best of all times to be married. One of my girl-friends said that once a woman has been asked, she shouldn't put it off one day longer than necessary.' Regina laughed. 'She speaks from experience; she lost her first love by being coy.'

He smiled at her. 'And you?'

'Next month, Harry?'

'Isn't that putting it off?'

They laughed, and moments later heard her uncle enter the house, stamp his feet as though he'd come in out of the rain, then come clumping towards the kitchen. Harry got off the stool for the second time.

Dr. Branch came in looking somewhat tired, but he greeted them both in his pleasantest voice and said jokingly he'd smelled Harry's pipe a square away, even before he saw the car out in front, and knew that he was there.

Harry's professional scrutiny inclined him towards the conviction that the Old Man had had a drink or two before reaching home. While the three of them spoke he reflected on that. No one became addicted to liquor in such a way that it became a physiological crutch in less than six or seven years of this kind of drinking. With healthy people, of course, the motivation frequently was so lacking that they didn't become alcoholics for fifteen years. But Dr. Branch had neither perfect health nor lack of reason for drinking a little each day, therefore he might be expected to become dependent upon the stuff a little sooner. On the other hand, when a man was past seventy years of age, it was a toss of a coin as to whether alcohol or death from normal causes claimed him first.

It wasn't pleasant to speculate about, but there it was. Hiding from facts never helped anyone; never altered those facts.

The Old Man kissed his niece, sniffed at what she was preparing, then asked if Harry was going to eat with them. When Regina said he was, Dr. Branch seemed pleased. He turned business-like then, and said, 'We've completed all the arrangements for the series of lectures, Harry.' His grey gaze lingered upon the younger man. 'They will require my presence at the college two days a week, perhaps even three days. Of course I cleared all that with the hospital board; they are agreeable, which is decent of them. But—this shifts a good deal of the burden to your shoulders, and that's what we must thrash out, I suppose.'

Harry had already known what the increased duties would entail and was reconciled. 'I'll draw on Belden and one or two of the others,' he said. 'It won't cause any hardship, I'm sure.'

The Old Man stood a moment in thoughtful silence, then said, 'I've been turning all this over in my mind lately, Harry. If I write that syndicated newspaper column, and engage in other series of lectures . . . It could result in me putting myself on the shelf, you know.'

Harry held his breath; he did not expect the Old Man to agree voluntarily to retirement even when it could be implemented by something he might be almost as fond of as he was of surgery. If the Old Man's next words indicated that he might actually consider retirement, most of Harry's secret anxieties would dissolve; would at least diminish in critical importance.

Dr. Branch said, 'It's certainly something to

consider isn't it?' and smiled at Harry, who was watching him. Behind the Old Man's back his niece was also watching but he didn't see that.

As though indicating that he didn't really take the remark about retirement seriously, Dr. Branch then said, 'Did you tell His Excellency he'd need surgery?'

Harry nodded. 'I told him. He took it fairly well. I might say he took it better than his physician did.'

Dr. Branch frowned. 'Oh yes, Dr. Haroush. I can imagine he didn't much like it. I've encountered that before; there is some kind of lingering anachronism in their country. If a doctor loses a patient he isn't considered much of a doctor.'

Harry was dry about that. 'I should rather imagine it's difficult for aged or ill people to find a physician to look after them. But in Dr. Haroush's case it has to be more than that. He gave me the impression that as a result of politics, if the Premier dies, Haroush might get his throat slit.'

Dr. Branch made an annoyed gesture. 'Those people and their damned politics. Harry, only a genuinely egotistical fool enters politics. Come along into the sitting-room where we can sit comfortably and discuss this forthcoming operation.' The Old Man turned. 'No offence, my dear. You can come along too if you'd like.'

She couldn't of course because there was the matter of getting their dinner. Harry let the Old Man walk out first, then slipped over and stole a kiss before he dutifully went out into the sitting-room.

There really was no innovation to discuss; both of them had participated in exactly this variety of exploratory surgery before.

They discussed different techniques, which was about all the leeway they'd be allowed, and talked about the Premier's physical condition as it related to what they would do to him. They didn't even speculate very much on the extent of the malignancy except when Dr. Branch said, 'If it's inoperable I think instead of simply closing him up and sending him home, we ought to let one of the team go along too. I have faith in Dr. Haroush, but this will, I believe be somewhat outside his ken.'

Harry was indifferent. If the malignancy was inoperable, then the best anyone, Haroush or someone from their own faculty, could do for Ibn Abdullah, was to keep him sedated until he died, praying always that it wouldn't be too prolonged a departure because of the body's ability to create resistance to numbing drugs.

Aloud he said, 'I looked at the schedules today. There will be opportunities tomorrow afternoon, the next morning, and the following afternoon again.'

Dr. Branch said, 'Tomorrow afternoon. Any objections?'

'None, sir.'

'Good. Then you can make the arrangements in the morning, eh?'

Harry agreed to see to that. 'Haroush should be allowed in.'

Dr. Branch shrugged. It wasn't important to him. He said, 'Harry, there's one other thing, before we stop talking shop tonight . . .' The Old Man's hawkish gaze went slowly to the younger man's face. 'One of the Renewal Board members was over at the college this afternoon; we had tea together.'

Harry felt the stare, thought he detected something critical or sceptical—or suspicious—in it, and sat like stone waiting for the Old Man to get to the point.

'He wondered if I'd consider replacing old Dr. Ames who is retiring this spring.'

Harry was so relieved he laughed, and it wasn't really anything very amusing. 'You accepted of course,' he said, and when Dr. Branch wrinkled his brow Harry said, 'You can't possibly refuse. Most of those procedures they use are your own ideas. There's no one alive, in my opinion, more eminently and thoroughly qualified.'

The Old Man seemed about to say something but Regina came to the door and smiled across the room. 'Unless you'd like to go on indefinitely discussing His Excellency's interior clockwork, we can eat.'

Harry rose. So did Dr. Branch. It was hard

to look at Regina and see such beauty and smiling warmth and think about Boards of Renewal, Premiers of countries, or anything else.

Regina's uncle said, 'Harry, has the date been set yet?'

He nodded, approaching Regina. 'Next month, sir.'

Old Dr. Branch started to nod, checked himself, looked down his nose and said, 'At the risk of seeming pedantic I'd like to point out that next month has thirty-one days to it.'

Regina stepped between them, hooked their arms with her hands and steered them to the candlelighted dining-room. 'The fifteenth,' she said to her uncle, then looked round. Harry nodded, squeezed her, and tried to think what was written in his appointment-book for the fifteenth of next month.

CHAPTER SEVENTEEN

THE IMPONDERABLES OF LUCK

The dinner was excellent; the conversation at the table and afterwards in front of the sitting-room fire again was also very good. Nothing was said about His Excellency, the Premier of Trans-Arabia and his crucial forthcoming operation, nor were any of the worrying things in any of their lives brought out to be discussed. Regina set the pace with a liveliness that kept her uncle and Harry Blaydon in high spirits as they matched wit for wit.

But towards nine-thirty Dr. Branch said he'd had a long day, had the prospect of an even longer one before him for the morrow, and thought he ought to be off to bed. He kissed his niece, praised her meal, winked at Harry and departed. The Old Man wasn't just being tactful by withdrawing his presence; he looked tired.

'He's kept it up too long,' murmured Regina, with quiet concern. 'He's past the age for driving himself so hard.'

Harry smiled. Some men understand no other purpose in life.' He thought a moment. 'Your uncle isn't the only man I've known who wanted to drop asleep the moment he hit a pillow.'

They went out to the dining-room and cleared the table. She was in half a mind to leave the dishes for the housekeeper but Harry talked her out of it. As she donned the little apron again he said, 'You must be aware that your chances of having the dinner dishes wiped surgically are extremely rare. If you don't avail yourself of my help I'm sure you'll regret it all your life.'

She laughed. 'You have no idea how I'll regret it,' she said, and rolled her eyes at him. 'But I doubt that it'll be so rare an event,

Doctor!'

He frowned, saying that she'd just made an ominous pronouncement and he was already having second thoughts about marrying her. 'You're only being sweet now for purposes of entrapment; after marriage I see myself becoming a slave to the sink.'

'No, not a slave actually, Doctor, but perhaps now and then a companion. Didn't you realise women do their best talking, and perhaps thinking too for all I know, in kitchens, usually while doing dishes?'

He feigned astonishment. 'Why hasn't this monumental revelation been included in the books on female psychology? Here may lie the secret to the entire female psyche. Imagine the vast popularity of a book saying the surest way to keep women content, satisfied, on a mental even keel, is to see that they do plenty of dishes.'

Her laughter rang out, and when he was concentrating on a large dish she leant and kissed his cheek. He smiled back but with both hands full could do very little else.

They didn't turn serious until they'd finished in the kitchen, strolled back to the sitting-room and he had begun stuffing his pipe in front of the fireplace. Then he said, I know what you are thinking about. Don't worry, after the briefing tomorrow I'll find some way to ease him off the surgical team.'

What Harry didn't say was that there would

be more pressure than just her opposition; he'd have to bow to it or face some kind of actual unpleasantness which he'd not be able to hide from her uncle.

'Are you so confident,' she wanted to know, 'that you can keep him away, Harry? After all, he is Chief Consultant, and doubtless most of the famous people who arrive at Memorial come there only because of his fame. Then there's his own ego, you know.'

He knew. He understood each of those points very well. His answer was down to earth. 'I'm afraid that if I don't find a way some others will find one for me. In any case, love, let's not worry about it tonight.'

'But have you any idea at all how to do it?'

He hadn't. That is, he could think of a dozen ways, but none of them were very subtle. What he told her was simply not to worry; that it would all resolve itself satisfactorily at the hospital in the morning.

She came to stand beside him in front of the fireplace and feel for his hand. She didn't find it because he slid it round her waist and said, 'So far we've been lucky. If our luck would only hold a bit longer . . .'

She amended that to say, 'If it had only been a little better luck, Harry. If only His Excellency hadn't turned up needing an operation until *he'd* been committed definitely at the college, or rendered unavailable in some other way.

That wasn't plausible but Harry refrained from pointing it out to her. After all, Dr. Branch was chief surgeon; his speciality had for years been just such people as His Excellency, Ibn Abdullah. It would have taken an awful lot of luck—or something—to keep the Old Man from performing the operation.

He led the conversation round to pleasanter channels by saying, 'I'll want him to give you away at the wedding, of course, and there'll be the matter of ushers and all. In fact, there's the matter of a church.'

She rallied, undoubtedly realising full well what he was doing, but she was agreeable; after all, this was the most serious, most exalted event of her life and nothing could have interfered with it for long.

'I've already made a mental note of bridesmaids' names. As for the church—I'll show you the one I'd like best the first time you have a day off.'

He led her to the sofa and they sat down together. He put his pipe aside, stole a sidelong peck at his watch, resolutely did not look at it again, and slid an arm round her shoulders, drawing her face over to be kissed. She turned soft and yielding in his arms. He said he still had trouble in believing so beautiful a girl could actually be interested in a grizzled surgeon whose lifelong dedication until the first time they'd kissed, had always been his work.

She smiled up at him. 'You're a very handsome man, Harry. Not in the movie-idol category, but that's in your favour. What women see in your face is strength, kindness, wisdom. As for you being a surgeon—I think it would have been very odd if I'd married out of the profession. That would have been rather like heresy. Imagine a cardinal's niece marrying a tennis player, or the niece of a farmer marrying a sailor.'

The fire burnt low, there was a good warmth inside the house, while outside the night advanced stealthily, giving as its only clue that this was so in the progress of a rising moon.

Neither of them knew nor cared whether the clouds had returned, whether the wind was building up again. Time was standing still in the huge room. She touched his face, traced the solid thrust of his chin and the lean lines of his lips, then put her head upon his shoulder and whispered of her love for him.

They sat like that for a long while before she finally lifted her face, sought his mouth and clung, working her lips upon his flesh. When he responded with a slow flash of passion she pushed clear and said, 'It's almost midnight, Harry. If you're drowsy tomorrow in conference my uncle will blame me.'

She straightened up, smiled, got to her feet and drew him up off the sofa. He didn't argue although he seemed not entirely willing. She led him out to the hall and there, after he'd kissed her good night, they parted.

He hadn't been very much aware of the lateness of the hour while in the cosy sitting-room but once on his way homeward it was borne in upon him by the silence of the streets he drove through, the lack of traffic, the off-centre position of that previously rising moon.

By the time he reached his flat it was nearly one o'clock in the morning, an unheard-of hour for him to still be up and wide awake unless out on an emergency call.

Even after he'd settled down in bed sleep took its time about arriving. His mind sprang from one subject to another until by sheer weight of responsibilities, he sank into slumber.

He awoke at the usual time feeling little the worse for something like six hours rest instead of eight, and left the flat to go out into a miraculously clear and sparkling morning which additionally heightened his sense of well-being. Not until he was driving through the unusual sunshine along with hundreds of other commuters did all his anxieties bear down upon him again.

But he was accustomed to responsibility; it was one of the strong points of his character that he could smile even though anxiety went every step of the way with him.

When he entered Memorial the first person he saw was Saud Haroush. The man looked

160

haggard. Harry sighed inwardly, greeted the physician and taking him by the arm entered the restaurant, which was just beginning to fill up with people. Haroush had little to say until Harry informed him that Dr. Branch had decided Ibn Abdullah would enter the operating theatre that afternoon. Then the black eyes widened and Haroush said, 'Of course; there must be no delay. And yet, I'm terrified of the results. Every omen points to something widespread and fatal.'

Harry had his coffee and toast. Haroush had only coffee. Dr. Belden went by, nodded, and didn't stop. Several other members of the staff did the same. Harry watched Belden with special interest. Had he by any chance met Andrew Connell the previous night?

Haroush finished his coffee and lit a cigarette. It was the first time Harry had ever seen him smoke. At the look Harry gave him the physician shrugged. 'A stimulant for me under some circumstances, a depressant under others. I don't smoke very often, though.' He regarded the cigarette clinically. 'Last night in my hotel room I also drank a good deal.'

Harry showed irritation. 'How do you feel now?'

Haroush made a little smile. 'Fine. As fine as I could under the circumstances. If you mean am I hung over, the answer is no. I didn't drink that much.'

That was precisely what Harry had meant.

He had nothing at all against a drink or two; he just did not approve of anyone being in a hospital, on a working basis or even as a patient who had been drinking or who was suffering from a hang-over.

He wanted to say something encouraging but didn't for the simplest of all reasons: there just was nothing at all encouraging one could say beyond reiterating what had already been mentioned about His Excellency's difficulty in being responsive to surgery. In the majority of cases it just was not true; even the odds were against it, which of course Haroush knew as well as Harry, but there was always hope. He mentioned that. Not with any amount of conviction in his voice, but simply in order to give Haroush something to cling to.

He also said, 'Doctor, there'll be a meeting this morning. If you will be available I'll take you in with me.'

Haroush was grateful. When Harry had finished his toast and coffee the physician caught the waitress's attention, picked up the bill and paid it himself as they left the crowded, noisy room.

On the way up to fourth floor he said, 'His Excellency gave me a letter last night. The one you suggested he dictate saying his condition was his own fault; saying that if he'd listened to me he would not be a dying man. I'm grateful for the forethought you had in that respect.'

Harry felt annoyed. 'He's *not* a dying man,

162

Doctor. I'd advise you against premature burial. There'll be plenty of time for that later, if it in fact becomes necessary.'

The statement reflected the difference between the fatalistic resignation of Saud Haroush, and Dr. Harry Blaydon, who would not—could not—accept any finality until every resource was first exhausted.

Haroush accepted the mild rebuke philosophically and when they parted outside Harry's office he said, with a little smile, 'His Excellency told me that if anyone could help him at all, it would be you. He is very grateful, Dr. Blaydon.'

Harry mechanically smiled, then entered the office, saw the neat, crisp pile of reports someone had placed there for his perusal, and sat down to face what had been his first routine function of the day ever since he'd come to Memorial.

As usual, some of the reports should have been sent to George Laxalt. Also as usual, he sifted these out, put them aside, and waded through what was left. One report held his attention longer than the others; it had to do with the kind of night the Premier of Trans-Arabia had spent, and it was encouraging. The old man had slept well, had drunk a glass of wine with his dinner, and had gone to sleep without a trace of fear.

Harry smiled to himself. If Saud Haroush had had as much iron in his constitution as the

163

Premier, he wouldn't have needed that liquor the night before. But of course if Haroush had been as strong as Ibn Abdullah, he, not the Premier, would perhaps have been leader of his country.

Emily rang at nine o'clock inviting Harry to Dr. Branch's office for a conference. He put everything aside, rose with a sense of resignation, and left the office.

CHAPTER EIGHTEEN

A TOTAL SURPRISE

Dr. Branch looked every inch the patrician patriarch in a dark suit and spotless linen as he led the team including doctors Belden, Blaydon, Carlson and Prothro into the conference-room that opened off his private office. Saud Haroush followed Harry Blaydon while Prothro and Carlson, quiet, solid men, brought up the rear.

There was both tea and coffee available on a sideboard but no one was interested in either as they all took seats round a highly-polished table and the Old Man sat down and placed a crisp folder he'd been carrying on the table in front of him.

Saud Haroush was the only outsider. He sat attentive and silent beside Harry. The room

164

was windowless and soundproof. Except for the opulence of its spartan furnishings—all expensive but unadorned—it would have somewhat resembled a large prison cell.

Dr. Branch began the meeting by giving a résumé of His Excellency's clinical history. The only time he glanced at Saud Haroush was when he'd finished with the résumé, then he waited just long enough for Haroush to nod approval before leaning back and saying, 'So it seems that short of explorative surgery we have no way of knowing just how long His Excellency's had this particular difficulty. Dr. Blaydon and I are hopeful without being optimistic.'

Up to this point Dr. Branch had said nothing none of the others weren't aware of. Harry, watching Norman Belden's face, tried to imagine what was running through the man's mind. Belden had one of those tight, long faces that seem always to border upon a scowl; it was therefore impossible for Harry to draw any very sound conclusions.

The Old Man then said, 'You gentlemen will comprise the surgical team. The main theatre will be used and the operation will take place this afternoon. Emily has already checked your schedules to make certain each of you will be available.' Dr. Branch paused, looking around. No one spoke. None of them even moved. They were concentrating on listening, for the moment. 'You know as well

165

as I do what we may encounter. You are also experienced in every facet of what will ensue regardless of the condition of His Excellency's stomach and other organs. I personally have not speculated; if we had more clues as to the length of time this condition has been critical, speculation might be possible. There are no such clues.

'Dr. Prothro, you will be the anaesthetist in charge. Dr. Carlson—in charge of the theatre Sister and assistants.'

Harry saw Norman Belden lean very slightly forward in his chair. It was so slight a movement that no one else appeared aware of it. Perhaps they wouldn't have been aware in any case because at this moment everyone was looking straight at Dr. Branch; this was the most critical part of any conference.

Harry had his answer, though, as to whether Belden had been contacted by Andrew Connell and that intermediary Andrew had mentioned. Belden *had* been contacted last night!

Harry's thoughts were wrenched back to the present by Albert Branch's next words. They were stated in the same cryptic, dispassionate tone of voice he invariably used at these meetings.

He said, 'Dr. Blaydon will operate and I shall assist.'

It was a hammerblow. Never before had Dr. Branch relegated the secondary post to himself. Always before Dr. Blaydon had assisted while Dr. Branch had performed the actual operation.

For five seconds no one spoke. Even when Dr. Carlson finally said, 'I presume Emily has worked up the chart for assistants and nurses.' Belden and Prothro, of course Harry himself, and even Dr. Branch, seemed held in the grip of that previous statement.

Dr. Branch nodded at Carlson. 'See Emily on your way out, Carlson.' He paused, let his eyes go from one of them to the other, let his glance linger a fraction longer on Norman Belden, then he said, 'Harry, remain behind a moment will you please? Gentlemen, unless there are questions the meeting is over. We'll meet in the operating theatre at twelve-thirty.'

They filed out. Norman Belden cast a glance down at Harry as he passed his chair but none of them said anything. At least two of them, Carlson and Prothro, probably had sensed no undercurrent even though they'd inevitably been surprised by the announcement that Blaydon, not Branch, would operate.

When the door was closed Albert Branch rose, got himself a cup of tea and returned to the table, all without a word. Harry filled his pipe but held it unlit. He was more interested in hearing what the Old Man had to say, when he eventually got round to saying it.

Branch took several swallows of the tea.

'Very good,' he murmured. 'You ought to try some, Harry. Oh, excuse me; I forgot you were a coffee man.'

Dr. Branch held up his hands. Even from the distance separating them which was two-thirds the length of the table, Harry saw the increased swelling, the unmistakable puffiness.

'Damned nuisance, isn't it?' said old Branch with a quaver of feeling in his voice. 'Look at them; I drove to work this morning surrounded by fishmongers, labourers, even thieves I suppose, and tried to find an answer as to why *these* hands that are so vital, so trained and skilled and needed, had finally to fail, when all those other hands would go right on selling fish or digging ditches, or picking pockets.'

He dropped the hands and gazed at Harry. 'Light your pipe. I enjoy the smell of good pipe tobacco.'

Harry obediently lit up, sat and regarded the older man. His private feelings were in turmoil. Fate had stepped in overnight and plucked the Old Man out of the exalted ranks. It was more than the luck he'd mentioned to Regina the night before, it was almost a miracle. But it was also something too deep for tears. Fifty years of polished surgical finesse at an end in one night.

He said, 'How bad is it?' and the Old Man grimaced at him.

'Too bad, Harry. Too bad to take the

chance.' Old Branch's dull eyes ironically brightened to the shade of cold steel. 'Startled Belden, didn't I?'

'Yes. And Carlson, Prothro—and me, too, sir,' replied Harry smiling softly.

'Well, it's done.'

Harry didn't know whether the Old Man meant his career as the nation's foremost surgeon was finished, or whether the decision, wrung from him no doubt at some cost, to step down and have Harry perform the operation, had amounted to an irreversible decision. He said, 'Nothing very much is changed, sir.'

Old Branch finished the tea, pushed the cup aside and leaned forward. 'Don't coddle me, Harry. You don't have to try and alleviate anything. What is it that makes us forever dream of immortality? I'm almost seventy-two years old. How much longer would I have lasted? You know damned well I've already gone nearly ten years longer than most of 'em do. And it's not just these cursed hands. Next summer it could have been my hearing, Harry, my eyes, muscular co-ordination . . !' The Old Man sank lower in his chair. Of course he knew that everything he had just said was perfectly valid, but on the other hand he was a proud man; it was extremely difficult for him to accept the finale.

He swore and straightened up a little, then forced a terrible smile. 'Well, how many hundreds have I looked squarely in the eye and known my skill wasn't going to add one damned lousy minute to their lives? And now it's my turn. But . . . my *hands,* Harry . . !'

A little buzzer flashed on the south wall where a series of lights linked the Conference Room with Dr. Branch's secretary's desk. Old Branch scarcely even looked up as Harry went across to the little grille and spoke his name. Emily said the Trans-Arabian Ambassador and an undersecretary from the Foreign office were waiting to see Dr. Branch. Harry thanked Emily and turned. Old Branch had heard, of course, and now rose from the table to smooth his coat and look thoughtful.

'You see,' he said, rallying, 'It could have been my tongue, Harry, in which case I'd have been unable to placate those two stooges out them. Why the devil didn't they wait until after the operation to ask their damned silly questions?'

As Dr. Branch preceded Harry from the room the younger man had a thought: *Yes, and it could have been your brain, and that would have been worst of all!*

Harry saw the two gentlemen in Dr. Branch's outer office. He nodded to both of them as he passed on into the wide, long corridor where, at this time of day, there was usually considerable activity.

Today was no exception. Nurses passed, several housemen were conversing in an undertone near the lift, and Dr. Saud Haroush was just emerging from the Premier's suite, but he didn't see Harry because he was looking intently at the floor.

Harry headed directly for his office. He reached it without being stopped, but five minutes later someone knocked and he resignedly looked up expecting either Haroush or Belden.

It was George Laxalt with an invitation to go to the restaurant for a late morning coffee-break. Harry declined and instead of departing, George draped himself into a chair. Harry promptly handed him the little stack of papers which should have gone to the Chief Administrator's office instead of the office of the Assistant Chief Consultant. George pulled a face, then dropped the papers to his lap and said, 'Some rather rare birds were in my cage earlier. An Ambassador and a—'

'Yes, I know,' broke in Harry. 'They're with the Old Man right now. I saw them on my way out.'

'Well, they have a suggestion, I think. I believe they want Dr. Branch to preserve His Excellency.'

Harry almost smiled. 'Do they now?'

George nodded, perfectly solemn. 'Yes, I gathered that it would be imprudent to have His Excellency die at this time.'

Harry laughed. Laxalt's humour was the kind that was never accompanied with a smile by its creator. George didn't so much as blink an eye now. He said, 'You will appreciate that His Excellency must not be permitted to exit, Dr. Blaydon.'

Harry said, 'Go and get your coffee, George. I've got to finish up in here, then have an early luncheon, and after that it will be time to join the other members of the carve and whittle club in the operating theatre.'

Laxalt rose in leisurely way, said, 'Good hunting,' and departed. He'd scarcely closed the door when Dr. Haroush entered, paused as though conscious of possible intrusion, then barged right in because Harry was only reaching for the telephone.

Harry looked at Haroush and slowly, very reluctantly, withdrew the reaching hand. 'I saw you coming from His Excellency's suite,' Harry said. 'I presume you told him of the meeting.'

'Yes. I also told him what Dr. Belden said to me as we left Dr. Branch's office—that this was the first time Dr. Branch had delegated the work of Chief Surgeon in all the years Belden had been at Memorial.'

Harry waited. There had to be more. Ibn Abdullah would have the last word. Haroush smiled and made a wide gesture with both hands.

'His Excellency said he approved; that although Dr. Branch was formidable, His Excellency was pleased to have a younger genius do the actual work.'

Harry was flattered. He was also amused at

172

Haroush's choice of words. He was hardly a genius; just a lifelong, highly trained specialist. He rose. 'Doctor, I'm a little pressed for time. If you will meet me in the operating theatre in an hour or so, we'll prepare. Meanwhile, will you excuse me?'

Haroush sprang up and held the door for Harry to pass through. Afterwards, Haroush closed the door and watched Harry stride briskly towards the lift. There, as the doors slid slowly closed, Harry and Haroush exchanged their last smile of the morning.

Harry went down to George Laxalt's office. 'Just give me ten minutes alone in here,' he said. 'That place of mine upstairs is worse than Piccadilly Circus. All the world and his wife marches in and marches out.'

Laxalt rose, made a gesture of extreme obeisance, and departed leaving Harry the private office—and the telephone—all to himself.

He at once dialled Regina. The telephone rang and rang and was never answered. Harry rolled up his eyes in quiet frustration, dropped into Laxalt's still-warm chair, and was about to try one last time when the instrument jangled. He reached for it and got a shock. Regina, on the other end, said, 'Harry, I'm in the restaurant keeping a table. Will you hurry along, love?'

He hung up and got up, his world turning bright and golden once more.

CHAPTER NINETEEN

REGINA DROPS A CLANGER

There was one flaw to their meeting. She'd evidently got her uncle's permission to use his private table, and that was quite all right, but no sooner had Harry greeted her and taken the chair opposite her than Norman Belden strolled into the restaurant, saw them and approached. Harry sighed with resignation; they weren't alone.

Belden gave Regina a smile and a little bow, both very gallant, then he turned his back on her and leaned down to say, 'At the eleventh hour, Harry.'

The man's pale, hard eyes didn't waver. Harry was annoyed. 'But you are satisfied,' he said, and Belden gravely inclined his head, so Harry then said, 'All right, Norman, now you can spy on me.'

Belden's head drew back just a little as though he'd been slapped. He was at a loss for words, evidently, because he leaned there as silent as a statue.

Harry glanced past, saw Regina watching them closely, and said, 'If you don't mind, Norman, we were about to have lunch.'

Belden straightened up, a thin shaft of antagonism in his glance. 'It never was a matter of spying and you know it,' he said sharply. 'It was just a matter of an imminent crisis.'

Harry smiled dryly at Belden's choice of words. 'Plus a little nudge from the outside,' he said.

Belden looked briefly surprised, but only briefly. 'What does that mean, Harry?'

'It means, Doctor, that last night you and a couple of other insufferable altruists met to play God.' Harry started to turn his attention back to Regina but Norman Belden's pricked pride interfered.

'Your laxity will some day make you just as vulnerable as *his* ego has made him!'

Belden turned and swiftly went over towards a distant table.

Regina, who'd heard it all and who had guessed what it all meant, looked a little anxiously across the table. 'You weren't very polite, love. He looked as though he'd been slapped.'

Harry said, 'If he'd hung around another couple of minutes that might have happened.' He looked round as the waitress appeared, all trace of annoyance gone from his features.

When they'd ordered Regina said, 'I know I couldn't have picked a worse day to visit Memorial.' He didn't dispute that; in fact he didn't say anything at all, so she went on. 'And I haven't gone up to see Uncle Albert; I just called Emily to ask how he felt this morning and ask whether we couldn't use this table for luncheon if we ate early.'

Something in her tone, her attitude, or perhaps inside his own brain, picked out one phrase—how he felt this morning—and closed down upon it. While Regina spoke he sat there looking at her, marvelling again, as he'd always marvelled, at her flawless beauty; at the clearness of the whites of her eyes and the creaminess of her complexion. Then he said, 'All right, sweetheart, let's have it.'

She looked suddenly startled—and guilty. Her eyes wandered away. He had a bad premonition. It dawned upon him what she'd done but he couldn't imagine how she'd managed it.

'Look, Regina; this has been a bad day for your uncle. I'm to perform the operation, he will assist—which means he'll be in reserve. It's not a position he's occupied, I'd guess, in perhaps a half century. We had a quiet little discussion after the conference this morning. He showed me his hands.'

'Saline,' she murmured. 'An overdose of concentrates, Harry.

He kept looking at her. She wilted under the stare, caught and held her lower lip between her teeth. Then he blew out a big breath and settled his arm upon the tabletop. It was the second hammerblow of the day.

She said, 'He explained how it worked one time, years ago when he first went on his salt-free diet.' She was near tears as she added, 'I feel like the most wretched traitor of all time. But ... Andrew called last night as I was getting into bed. He said he'd just come from a very serious meeting with a member of the staff here at Memorial, and another physician. They were going to get an injunction against him this morning. Harry? What else could I have done?'

For a moment Harry turned and gazed over to Norman Belden's table. He looked as though he might jump up, go over and do something rash. But the expression passed, he turned and said, with a gentle nod, 'You did right, love. It was a hell of a difficult position for Belden and Connell to put you in, but you did just exactly right. Fortunately your uncle will be too busy for the rest of the day to carry out tests on himself, if he suspects anything, and by night when he'll have the time, the residue should be dissipated.'

Their food came and neither of them did more than pick at it. She wanted to know if her uncle was in pain.

Harry shook his head. 'He's taken an injection to alleviate that. But he showed me his hands this morning. I was surprised at such deterioration; normally the process is very gradual, up to a point at any rate, and then of course its progress is faster, but by then there is partial crippling.'

'But you guessed, Harry.'

177

He couldn't explain that without making a very unprofessional judgement so all he said was, 'Belden was correct when he said Dr. Branch had abdicated at the eleventh hour.'

'And now you will perform the exploratory?'

That didn't bother him, he'd done others of the same nature. Not, it was true, on such an exalted personage, but as he privately told himself, all men were the same under an anaesthetic on an operating table.

'Nothing to worry about there,' he told her, and reached for his coffee cup. An idea struck him, 'Are you booked up for the afternoon?' She shook her head, pale and still distraught. 'Fine. Then I'll take you back to my office and you can wait there for me. It may be a rather prolonged wait though, so perhaps you'd rather go shopping or something, and meet me at the office about four this afternoon.'

She said, 'I'll wait. Harry? What if Uncle Albert finds out?'

He didn't think that was very likely and told her so, then, his appetite coming back, he ate part of his lunch, saw Dr. Belden rise and leave the room from the corner of his eye, glanced at his wrist, and lifted his napkin. It was time to go.

'Don't worry,' he told her, reaching over to hold her hand across the table. 'Your uncle won't find out. Maybe some day we can tell him—explain about Andrew and all the rest—but for the moment, don't worry. He won't be

178

in any danger of being discredited, and I'll perform the operation without difficulty. It is, after all, fairly routine.'

He rose. She didn't move from her chair. She looked wan and tired. He almost suggested that she should go home and take a nap but she wouldn't have done it so he simply bent, kissed her cheek, then turned and started out of the room. He was too preoccupied to notice the looks of astonishment on the faces of several young housemen at a nearby table.

In fact, until he stepped out of the lift on the fourth floor and met Norman Belden almost face to face, he wasn't very conscious of much of anything around him.

Belden jerked up stiffly and turned to walk away. Harry said, 'Norman, come in the office with me for a moment.' It was more an order than a request. Belden dutifully followed along, closed the door after himself and even took the chair Harry motioned him to take.

Harry was blunt. 'Listen; I don't give a damn what you think of me, but there's something that's got to be thrashed out. Dr. Branch will be at the college a good deal of the time from now on. He'll very likely be doing a syndicated column for a newspaper, and also there've been feelers from other institutions about his willingness to give other series of lectures. That means I'll be Chief Consultant. It also means, since you have both the seniority and the ability, you'll be moving into my present position as Assistant Chief Consultant.

'Norman, if we can't get along it's going to play hell with morale. So it's going to be up to you. I'm certain you can find another position with equal status and even more money. If that's your wish, I'll do everything I can to help you make the change.'

Dr. Belden's thin, long face reddened slightly. He was a forthright man himself, but since Harry was normally tactful, this sudden eruption of total candour must have stung Belden a little. He stood up, went over to a bookcase, turned his back to it and stared at Harry. 'You know perfectly well I've been right about the Old Man all along, Harry.'

Harry agreed. 'You have.'

'And if I've done anything improper perhaps it was because I just haven't your tact.'

Harry glanced at his watch. Time was running out.

Norman, I'm not making any accusations. I'm simply pointing out some hard facts to you.'

Belden inclined his head slightly, stiffly, then said, 'I don't know how you found out I met Connell last night, but that's not very important anyway, is it?'

Not important at all. Andrew also believes he was right. And in substance he most certainly was. In practice he was more gadfly than helper.'

'All right, that description will fit me also, but in case you're interested, Harry, I refused to go along with him on that injunction. It's unethical. When he became irate I told him that both you and I would be there today in the operating theatre and if the Old Man so much as faltered we would move in. Was I right?'

'You were.'

'All I meant when I mentioned that the Old Man'd waited until the eleventh hour to disqualify himself was that I was tremendously relieved.'

Belden stepped over to the desk and thrust out a hand. Harry gripped it, and smiled. Belden didn't smile back. He said, 'We'll work together very well. I've envied your calmness and talent ever since you arrived here. I can't imagine anyone more qualified to step into the Old Man's boots, Harry. That's not meant as flattery at all, it's simply my statement of fact.'

Harry knew Belden well enough to know the zealot wouldn't permit a word of flattery to pass his lips if his life depended upon it.

'It's well after noon,' he said. 'I suggest we go up the hall.'

They were met outside the office by Dr. Haroush who had evidently been patiently waiting. Belden nodded to the younger and smaller man and then went away. Harry took Haroush by the arm.

'You're looking better,' he said quietly, and

181

the physician smiled gratefully.

'I have exhausted all the feelings except that particular one,' he said.

Dr. Branch was speaking outside his office with the two dignitaries who'd been in there waiting to see him for an hour and more. Harry was surprised that they were still there.

There was a small knot of quiet, busy people in the large washroom when they entered. A few looked up, a few smiled at Harry, but otherwise no one seemed to notice the advent of the remainder of the team. Doctors Carlson and Prothro were being assisted into surgical gowns by a couple of husky housemen.

Harry and Belden scrubbed up side by side, neither speaking until, near the end of their scrupulous ablutions Dr. Belden leaned and said in a whisper, 'I think it might be as well if we put someone either beside Dr. Haroush or behind him. He looks like a fainter to me.'

Dr. Branch was late getting to the scrub-room. He said to Harry, with an annoyed scowl, that if all diplomats had to do was talk, he wished they'd practise their oratory somewhere else.

But of course he was perfectly accustomed to this kind of interruption. It did not sit well with him, and one was free to imagine that ten or twenty years earlier Dr. Branch wouldn't have demonstrated the patience he'd shown today.

A nurse with grey hair, sparkling brown eyes and a handsome figure, poked her head in to say, 'Dr. Prothro, the patient is here.'

Prothro, as anaesthetist, nodded and left the room. The first step in a long, tense afternoon's work had just been taken.

CHAPTER TWENTY

THE OPERATION

The operation was, as Harry had told Regina, routine. Of course it was impossible for any of that silent, skilled team of men and women not to be conscious of the prestige of the man being worked upon. But as far as outward flap was concerned, there was none.

Harry, Norman Belden and Albert Branch were down prior to the initial incision. They conferred in low, brusque tones. His Excellency was a muscular man, elderly it was true and therefore with the lack of skin-tone one found in younger people, but evidently at one time in his life he'd been as strong as steel. This of course was in his favour now; there was no fat to snip away. He was as inert as clay while Harry bent to his work.

Saud Haroush, relegated to a distant position, wiped his fore-head with an immaculate white handkerchief and Belden, who was too otherwise occupied, failed to note this. But Haroush didn't show that he might faint although he looked quite pale.

There was a large electric clock on a wall whose severely plain and functional black hands moved infinitesimally although the sweeping second-hand kept up a constant and regulated circling movement. From time to time someone would glance at this clock.

However, this operation was not being performed against time as was so often the case; this time there was no haemmorhage, no faltering heart, to contend with. As Harry had said, it was largely routine.

Dr. Branch moved just once; that was to turn and raise an eyebrow in the direction of Carlson who was co-ordinating his efforts with those of Dr. Prothro. Carlson looked steadily back and gave a slight nod of reassurance. After that the Old Man stood opposite Harry watching the other man's strong, sure hands.

Dr. Belden leaned to look when Harry exposed the injured organ, his pale eyes narrowed to a honed sharpness; this was where Norman Belden shone best. He had a mind as sharp as any scalpel in the room. He also had the experience and judgement that made a sound assessment probable. But he said nothing.

None of them did. Not at the time Harry probed around the diseased organ searching for the deadly growth's terminus.

The Old Man was like a stone statue, only his eyes moving, as Harry worked. He too had the diseased tissue in sight. When Harry straightened up and looked at the other two, the three of them seemed to communicate through sight alone. Harry smiled but because the lower part of his face was hidden it showed only around the puckered eyes. Neither colleague smiled back although Belden nodded his head which might have meant agreement with whatever Harry had in mind, or it might have simply been a sign of encouragement.

This was the moment for a hurried conference, but these men had been through this many times before, they knew precisely what had to be done. They also knew Harry intended to do it. There wasn't a word said.

Dr. Carlson bent low to make a visual check of His Excellency's visible breathing, then turned to check that against the dials near at hand. He and Dr. Prothro used the same silent means of communication; Prothro, also made a visual check and nodded. Carlson transmitted this information by way of a hand lightly pressed upon the Old Man's arm.

Harry went to work on the removal. His movements had the strength, the sureness, of full confidence. The fact that a man's life was now at stake seemed not to occur to him. He was quite calm in his probing and incising.

The clock on the wall was forgotten by

everyone except Dr. Haroush who consulted it from time to time with an increasing expression of anguish. As a physician he was familiar with the general techniques of surgery, but as a man whose personal destiny was linked closely with the destiny of that man lying as if dead upon the operating table, he was torn by anxiety and dread. He must be aware that the length of time a person spent under the knife was in direct ratio to the slowness of recovery after surgery; for a young man, of course, the experience, traumatic though it invariably was, posed far less of a peril than for a man as old as His Excellency.

Haroush was being torn apart inside. Of all the people in that room, barring of course the patient himself, Haroush's recovery would be slowest and most painful. It could have been said of him that although he was physically endowed for general medicine, he definitely was not constituted for the exigencies of surgery. It was a common enough condition among general practitioners. But he was an outsider; the surgical team in the room with him, from much-honoured Albert Branch to gifted, wise and confident Harry Blaydon, from thorough and skilled Norman Belden to the nurses, had been chosen out of a talented complement; they were the best in the land at their work. As a team, they worked as quietly and efficiently as was humanly possible.

Time did not work on their side but they'd

perfected adequate techniques that could almost arrest the passing of time. There probably was no better surgical team in all the world, although there may have been other teams just as seasoned and talented.

Harry's cap showed a dark stain where it fitted snugly upon his forehead. His usually calm and amiable eyes began to assume a fixed, squinted expression. He worked without glancing up, both hands moving with a thorough deftness. Finally, when he raised his eyes and straightened up, Norman Belden went round to stand beside him. Harry moved back and with scarcely any waste of time or motion Belden moved in for the closure. This was Belden's speciality. Experienced in all aspects of his work, Belden's present assignment was what he was doing now, and what he did best.

Harry turned away. There were two more of those dark stains now, at each armpit. It was cool in the room but nothing could have prevented tension from getting to the chief surgeon, and Harry Blaydon had been chief throughout.

Dr. Branch watched Belden briefly, then raised his eyes to watch Harry. His gaze was as pitiless now as Norman Belden's gaze always was. He was studying Harry Blaydon in the aftermath of an exhausting ordeal; it was as important for a surgeon's nerve to remain like steel afterwards as it was for it to be so during an operation.

Harry waited a moment, ducked his head slightly for a nurse to pat his face with a cool cloth, then he stepped over for a last look at Belden's work, and finally turned to leave the theatre.

Dr. Branch's gaze followed him all the way out of the room, but the Old Man stood fast, still in his supervisory capacity, responsible for the last stitch.

For Harry it was over. He let a houseman help him out of the surgical gown. He scrubbed up at a wash-basin and looked at his face in the mirror. He was tired-looking around the eyes and grim around the mouth. It was a familiar look; he never went through an operation without feeling completely wrung out. The sensation sometimes lasted all the rest of the day. Sometimes, if the operation were performed in the early morning, he was recovered by mid afternoon. Today, it was already late afternoon. He knew he'd fall asleep by eight o'clock unless he had a pick-me-up.

Saud Haroush appeared in the room. Harry saw him over his shoulder as he stood gazing into the mirror at his own haggard reflection. He had to reach far down for the strength to use in meeting the battery of questions sure to come. He hadn't a great deal of strength left.

But Haroush surprised him. Although undoubtedly crawling with anxiety, the physician walked up and gently patted Harry's shoulder. He said, 'His Excellency has always been a superb judge of men. He would have been very pleased today.'

Harry began drying hands and arms as he turned. 'He won't feel much like cheering for a day or two. But if you see him before I do you can tell him that taking care of his health as a young man was very much in his favour today.

They left the wash-room together. Harry felt in a pocket for his wristwatch, glanced at its hands as he slipped it on, and saw George Laxalt eyeing him as he headed for his office. George had an unpleasant duty now; he had to get a definitive statement. Harry waved at George to tag along. Laxalt did.

When Harry entered the office expecting to find Regina there, the place was empty. He felt a sudden lowering of the spirit. It had been the thought of seeing her that had sustained him. But there was a little note propped against his silver pen. He picked it up, read it while both Laxalt and Haroush waited, then he smiled and, slipping the note into his pocket, dropped down and said, 'Chairs, gentlemen. As for statements—you know the rule, George. We'll wait until Dr. Branch gets here.'

Then he did a startling thing; he opened a low deskdrawer, set up a bottle of scotch, set up three small glasses and poured them partly full without saying a word. As he handed them over he said, 'There is no place in a hospital

189

for social drinking. Even medicinal drinking shouldn't be encouraged. But this, gentlemen, is sacramental drinking, and that is entirely different. To His Excellency, Ibn Abdullah, Premier of Trans-Arabia, may he live to be a hundred and ten!'

They drank. Harry afterwards searched the desk for a pipe, found one under a pile of untidy papers, filled it and lit up. Saud Haroush took this as tacit permission for him to light a cigarette. George Laxalt wrinkled his nose.

'That was very good scotch,' he said, 'but what, may I ask, are you gentlemen smoking—old socks?'

They sat in silence for a long time. It grew uncomfortable after a while but Harry made no move to end it. He was contentedly sitting there letting the alcohol reinforce his physical resources as the slow business of recovery and regeneration went on.

Fifteen minutes later Dr. Branch and Dr. Belden walked in. Haroush and Laxalt at once sprang up. There were only three occasional chairs in the office. The Old Man ignored that gesture of respect and stepped across to plant himself with his back against a tall bookshelf. This was his moment; he'd lived through many hundreds just like it, but each one was different. He looked at Harry.

'Excellent,' he said. That was the highest praise he ever offered. Words such as 'marvellous' 'fabulous' 'inspiring' he left to newsmen. 'Excellent, Dr. Blaydon; you carried it off perfectly.' He looked over at Norman. 'Any comments on that, Dr. Belden?'

'None, sir, unless I say I thoroughly agree with your appraisal.'

The Old Man took his time. He glanced at Haroush—on the edge of his chair—and George Laxalt, who'd been through this every week for several years and was interested without being apprehensive. George always hoped for a good report; he had to phrase it for the press; but he could at least be detached which was something none of the others could be.

The Old Man said, 'What was your judgement, Dr. Blaydon?'

'Minor, isolated malignancy, sir, which probably did not contribute very much to His Excellency's pain; it must have been that ulcerated segment I removed along with the malignancy.'

Haroush collapsed back into his chair. Tears welled up and the other men, embarrassed for him, did not look.

George loosened too, but for different reasons. 'Is that final, doctors?' he asked. 'Should I put it like that for the newsmen?'

The Old Man said, 'Report the surgery as an unqualified success, George, without details. Say that His Excellency, barring complications, will be able to leave Memorial within two weeks, if he chooses to do so.' The Old Man permitted himself a small smile. 'Don't clear it with me when you've written it up, clear it with Dr. Blaydon. Well, Norman . . . ?'

Belden nodded complete approval. He even permitted himself one of those extremely rare and not too delightful smiles of his.

George Laxalt sat a moment, caught Harry's eye, slowly winked, then rose to depart. Saud Haroush also started to rise. Harry gestured for him to remain where he was.

Moments later, after a little shop-talk between the three surgeons, the Old Man and Dr. Belden left.

Harry blew out a great sigh, smiled and got up to reach for his over-coat. 'You and I,' he said, 'are going for a little drive, Doctor. First I have to pick up my fiancée, who left me a note saying she waited in here as long as she could, then went down to the church several doors from Memorial to pray for our success. After that the three of us will go somewhere quiet, have a few drinks and a decent dinner. Then, of course, we'll see you home. Agreed?'

Haroush sprang up with the look in his eyes a dog shows only to its master.

CHAPTER TWENTY-ONE

THE OLD MAN'S ULTIMATE DECISION

They had no difficulty in finding Regina. She almost ignored Saud Haroush as she stood looking anxiously at Harry. He said, 'I believe your prayers were answered.'

They all went back to the car. There was a gusty wind blowing, cold and disagreeable. It was dark out with lights of all colours and shades forming a bulwark against the lowering night.

Harry drove to a small restaurant he frequented because it was quiet, off the beaten path, and served excellent meals. He led his guests to a shadowy corner table and when a waiter appeared ordered a round of drinks. Then he leaned upon the table and said, 'His Excellency's ulcer was a blessing in disguise. What he'd thought had to be a pain connected with something else, turned out to be the ulcer spreading. There was a malignancy distinctly recognisable as not being a benign tumour—and it was removed. The ulcer was also taken care of. Of course the biopsy will determine whether my diagnosis concerning the cancer is correct or not.' Harry moved to permit his drink to be set in front of him. Then he said, 'Of course there is always some danger of diseased cells breaking off and spreading through the body. But I believe, even if this happens, we can stop the cancer completely. That will require constant check-ups over a period of four years.' He smiled at Haroush. 'But I should imagine His Excellency won't mind undergoing that inconvenience since it means he'll still be around for the next four years. Something I'm sure he did not believe last night.'

Regina offered a toast to His Excellency. Haroush and Harry dutifully drank, then the physician said, 'Miss Branch, this is a very strong drink. If I have any more toasts to drink to His Excellency's health, I may ruin my own.'

They ordered food and when Regina suggested another drink the men smiled at one another; they knew something she had no inkling of—they were already a large glass of straight scotch ahead of her.

As both men declined Regina had only that one drink. When the food came Harry noticed the first signs of exhaustion moving in. A second drink now would only increase the drowsiness. Of course the meal would do the same thing. He told himself there just was nothing for it, unless it was a long walk in the chill night air, and resumed eating while the other two carried most of the conversation between them.

Later, when they were outside again, the cold air brightened Harry's spirit. He drove

Saud Haroush to the hotel where he was staying, accepted his gushing thanks, promised to see the physician the following day, then turned instinctively towards his own flat.

Regina didn't comment. She put her head upon his shoulder and silently watched as headlamps approached, then passed by again.

About the time they pulled up in front of the block of flats a few small beads of wind-whipped rain fell upon Harry's windscreen. He shook his head; being accustomed to vile weather did not especially ensure that one became fond of it. He turned and asked if Regina was awake. She sat up smiling, looked out of the window, looked at him and said, 'What will the neighbours think, you bringing me to your flat in the night like this?'

'They ought to be used to it by now; anyway, they'll all be glued to the telly tonight. Ordinarily the thing disgusts me, but on nights like these last few have been I think it's better than an electric blanket.'

They left the car and ran inside. Those raindrops were fatter now; also, they were falling with a steadier constancy. In the flat where they both shed coats and hats, Harry switched on his transistor radio. He let it make its ceaseless noise only until a weather report came on, then switched it off. There was no rain predicted.

He took Regina out to the kitchen—where a forlorn dinner sat, left as usual by the housekeeper—and set about making them both a cup of coffee. The little dining-annexe out there consisted of a small table next to the window, and two chairs. That's where they sat gazing out into the rain that shouldn't have been falling, while she asked questions about her uncle.

Harry hadn't had much to say to the Old Man after the little news conference in his office. He thought by then the swelling in her uncle's hands would have been considerably lessened. 'Salt is one of the things the human body absorbs fastest.'

She said, gazing out into the dismal night, 'I'm almost afraid to face him.'

He drank off his coffee and poured a second cup. She had only the one cup; actually, she didn't much care for the stuff, having been a tea-drinker since childhood.

As he sat down again he said, 'I am more pleased with the results of the operation for Haroush's benefit than for the Premier's. Haroush aged five years today.'

She looked at him. 'Dr. Haroush will survive. You seem confident His Excellency will too. That leaves Uncle Albert—and us.'

He grinned at her. 'No danger of we two not surviving. As for your uncle, he has every reason to go right on earning laurels. Not in surgery, that's all.'

'He may not be willing to assist next time, Harry.'

'He will, love. When we talked this morning after the operation, I think I saw all the signs I was looking for. I'm sure Belden also did. But I'll have another talk with him in the morning.'

A bell rang. Harry got up, heading for the telephone first, then veered as the doorbell made its insistent sound the second time. He had a look on his face as though to ask who on earth would be visiting at this time of night, and on as stormy and unpleasant a night as well.

When he opened the door he had occasion to blink. So did Regina who was looking round the doorless entrance to the kitchen and dining-annexe. It was her uncle with a coat draped round his thin shoulders and his hat tugged so low he resembled some caricature of a gangster.

He stepped inside, saw his niece and made a little pecking nod in her direction. 'God, what a night,' he said, handing hat and coat to Harry. He smelled of wind and rain. Harry wasn't too sure he didn't also smell slightly of alcohol, but there was one thing he'd noticed; the Old Man never showed in the slightest that he'd been nipping.

Harry got him a cup of coffee, which he drank sweetened, and the three of them moved into the sitting-room. After a bit the Old Man said, 'George, I'd have made the move anyway, you understand, but after today I've decided to resign as Chief Consultant at

Memorial.'

Both Harry and Regina were thunderstruck. They had expected some change, of course, because inevitably there had to be some, but they certainly had never even discussed the Old Man actually stepping out. Memorial Hospital had been his love, his family, his creation, his life.

He considered their stunned expressions and bleakly nodded. A rush of wind-driven rain smashed against a window.

Harry said, 'There's no reason, sir.'

'There's every reason, my boy. In the first place I'm finished as a surgeon. You and I both know that. Today only clinched it, but we've both known this was coming for some time. So did you, Queenie. So did Andrew, although confound him, he had to keep rubbing my nose in it. In any case, if I hung on another six months or another year, what difference could that make? On the other hand, as you saw today, Harry, my failure might be terrible—not just for me, but for some poor devil under surgery.'

He rose and paced across to the window where the rain was beating against the panes. Actually, the measure of his distraught condition was obvious in the fact that not all his sentences were related as he shot them at his listeners. He gazed out into the bitter night a moment then turned, hands thrust deep into pockets.

'I've taken the liberty of recommending you as my successor, Harry. No, don't say anything just yet! I had a long session with the Board of Governors this evening.

I called it as a special meeting—executive session, they call it. I recommended you as Chief Consultant Surgeon and Norman Belden as Assistant Chief.

'Now then, if you believe I had no business to do that without first consulting you—you are perfectly right, I hadn't. But you are the only one I'd recommend, and it'll be up to the Board to persuade you to accept.

'As for me, well, I'll remain as emeritus consultant. Harry; it has to be this way. I haven't dedicated all these years to Memorial only to see it deteriorate when I do. It will be my monument. I don't want anything ever to detract from its world-wide reputation. Neither will you.'

The Old Man went back and slumped down again. He looked at his niece as though he might address her separately, but in the end he simply leaned far over and patted her tenderly.

Harry felt guilty and ashamed of himself. He hadn't plotted against the Old Man to get the Chief's position, but it would most certainly appear that way to anyone else. It even looked a little like that to him, at this very moment.

But the Old Man was right on all counts; Harry should succeed him, Belden should move into Harry's position, and the Old Man should be carried on the Memorial roster as surgeon emeritus. He was right in what he'd said about the hospital. It was internationally famous and with full justification. It should not be allowed to deteriorate simply because the man who had made it what it now was, had grown too old to remain at the helm.

It was not a very pleasant time for Harry despite the increase in prestige which would shortly be his. He said, 'It is entirely up to you, sir. If you would prefer to recommend some new man from outside Memorial for the Chief Consultant's post, I'll most certainly serve him as I've served you.'

Dr. Branch said, 'Nonsense, Harry. Humility is all good and well but don't waste it on me. I'm not a humble man, never was; I believe in holding one's head up, doing one's absolute, unqualified best, and the devil take the hindmost.' Then he smiled. 'All right, it's all settled between us then. The Board will call you in to see them tomorrow. You can do as you wish. You have all night to think about it.' He rose. 'And I'll save you the bother of driving Queenie home, she can go back with me.'

Harry and Regina looked at one another. They'd only been at the flat a short while; neither of them wished to part with the other yet.

Dr. Branch picked up his coat, settled his

hat upon the back of his head and struggled into his coat grimacing as he did so; the arthritis injection had all but worn off, raising his arms was beginning to be painful again.

'Damned ailment anyway,' he muttered as Harry and Regina moved to help. 'But this way it bothers *me*, you see, and suppose senility had crept in; then that would have bothered everyone.' He turned, straightening the coat. 'Harry, you've got to accept, you know. You're my last link with Memorial. If a perfect stranger took over I just wouldn't feel that I had any right to walk in over there.'

'You'll keep your office, won't you?' asked the younger surgeon, and the Old Man adamantly shook his head.

'Not at all. As an emeritus I won't need an office. Moreover, I've got my office at home. It's better suited for writing lectures, preparing newspaper columns and so forth, anyway. And Emily will come with me, of course. We'll be busy enough, I foresee. Perhaps too busy.'

He reached, held the younger man's hand for just a moment in a very rare show of feeling, then, seeming embarrassed that he'd shown emotion, he said, 'Kiss him goodnight, Queenie; the man's been on his feet all day. He needs rest. Kiss him and let's get along home. It's been a hell of a day for me too.'

She obeyed. She clung to Harry as her uncle marched out into the hall to wait discreetly beyond sight.

He felt the salt tears on his cheek as she burrowed her face into his shoulder after the kiss. He squeezed her wordlessly, then took her to the door.

'I'll ring you at home,' he promised. 'I love you, Regina.'

After she and her uncle had gone, Harry closed the door, turned to look at the empty room, and finally rubbed his eyes because they were beginning to smart with weariness.

He didn't bother to clear away the coffee-cups, but went instead to shower and climb into bed. True to prediction, his head no sooner touched the pillow than he was asleep.

Too much had happened; he'd been overwhelmed by it all. Sleep was the best of all interludes when stress and strain pulled a man one way, then another way.

Outside, the blustery night with its fitful lashes of rain began to diminish in force. By morning the storm would be past and gone.

CHAPTER TWENTY-TWO

AN END TO ALL QUESTIONINGS

Harry still felt a little groggy even after a good night's rest. When he arrived at the hospital and went to have his morning cup of coffee he hadn't even noticed that a wet and dripping world was being dried out by a bright sun which hung suspended just above the rooftops.

The air was cleansed, there was a freshness to it only someone entirely wrapped up in their own thoughts could avoid noticing. Harry missed it.

He also missed seeing Norman Belden over on the other side of the large restaurant at a table with Carlson and Prothro. After the coffee had livened him up a bit he took the lift to the fourth floor and headed for his office to do the routine thing he'd been doing for several years—sort out and examine the reports of the night staff. Only when he came to the pages devoted to His Excellency, Premier Ibn Abdullah, did he relax, lean back and read slowly.

His Excellency had spent a fairly good night; he'd been a little restless towards morning which was to be expected but otherwise his condition seemed to be steadily and surely improving. Harry was gratified; he made a mental note to go round perhaps late in the afternoon and see the Premier. Until then it was doubtful whether His Excellency would have enough interest in anything to care whether he was going to live or die.

Then too there was the matter of working up charts for Dr. Haroush outlining what His Excellency could, and could not, eat, from here on. After all, one did not lose a portion of one's stomach and go right back to spiced curry and the like.

Otherwise, the reports were routine.

There was a memo from George Laxalt, time-stamped shortly after Harry had departed the evening before, to the effect that a government official had called asking for something more detailed and definite than the short piece George had passed out to the newsmen. George wanted Harry to write up such a memo, providing Harry and the Old Man agreed the government was entitled to it.

Harry stuffed that memo into a pocket and reached for the telephone to confer with Dr. Branch. Emily said he hadn't come in yet but she'd ask him to ring back. He broke the connection without replacing the telephone, raised the little button after a moment and dialled Regina. He didn't expect to get the Old Man but he did, so he smoothly moved into a conversation relative to the note from Laxalt. Dr. Branch said he was about to leave, would think it over on the drive down, and would see Harry then.

Harry at once asked if he might speak to Regina. The Old Man chuckled. 'I didn't really believe you wanted me anyway.'

Regina spoke with a little pleased sound to her voice. In the background Harry heard her uncle teasing her, then the door slammed which meant the Old Man had left the house.

He said, 'I keep thinking about you. Do you suppose it might become a fixation and I'll need psychiatric care?'

Her answer was warm. 'You'd better keep thinking about me. As for the psychiatrist—let me suggest the proper therapy.'

He laughed. She made him feel ten years younger and carefree. 'Could we perhaps have dinner out this evening? Providing of course your uncle, His Excellency the Premier of abracadabra, or some other immensely important bigwig doesn't pop up in the meantime.'

'If they do, Doctor,' she said at once, 'hand them over to Dr. Belden—or the janitor—but don't you turn me down. I'll be expecting you at seven.'

He agreed to the time, rang off, and was still smiling when George Laxalt rang him up. He very neatly shed the entire business of what to tell the public relations man by telling George the Chief Consultant would soon arrive, and George should buttonhole him on the topic.

He then rose to get out of the office before the telephone rang again. He made it, only to walk almost into the arms of Dr. Haroush, fresh-looking and bright-eyed.

He called Harry something garbled in his native language that probably was flattering, but one never knew, then suggested they go together to see His Excellency. Harry demurred on good grounds.

'He'll still be under the weather. Why not let him rest until late this afternoon?'

Haroush made a surprising statement. 'No, Doctor, His Excellency is in fine condition. I just left him to come down here and bring you back with me, at his orders.'

It was an amazing improbability. The man'd had major surgery not more than twelve or fourteen hours earlier. Harry said, 'You just left him, and he was fully in control of himself, mentally?'

Haroush smiled. 'Come and see for yourself.' He took Harry's arm but the surgeon still resisted.

'I really can't answer his questions until Dr. Branch is here.'

Haroush made a disdaining gesture. 'I have already told him everything.'

Harry eyed the smaller man pensively. It was on the tip of his tongue to remark that if Haroush had told His Excellency 'everything' then Haroush had to know a lot more than anyone else knew at Memorial. The results of the biopsy wouldn't be known until much later in the day. Until that report was in hand no one could say with absolute certainty that the malignancy had not spread.

Haroush seemed to read some of Harry's thoughts because he said, giving the arm he held a sharp tug, 'Doctor, whatever ensues His Excellency says you have granted him another four years; he told me there is no way to put a price on something as precious as time. If, after the four years have passed, he must then die, he told me he was perfectly willing. Now will you come?'

Harry went, but primarily because it seemed inconceivable to him that His Excellency could be sufficiently recovered already, to indulge in philosophical observations.

His Excellency was as pale and lifeless as a corpse when they stepped silently into his room. His dark eyes, sunken now and shiny, seemed the only part of him imbued with life, or any will to go on living. Two special nurses moved discreetly back as Harry went towards the bed and smiled at the sick man. He took Ibn Abdullah's pulse, found it quite satisfactory all things considered, and drew up a chair to sit down. He was still surprised to find Ibn Abdullah totally rational. He'd survived a tremendous physical and psychological shock. It had to be that indomitable will in the older man's body that had made such an unusual recovery possible.

The Premier said in a low, fading voice, 'Dr. Blaydon; I am informed the operation was a great success.' The dark, fatalistic eyes showed faint irony. 'Of course the one who said that had his reasons for praying this all might be so. What do *you* say?'

Harry told the Premier what he'd encountered, what had been removed, and scrupulously avoided being too hopeful. It was a somewhat trite little recitation; Harry even blushed a little for himself. Ibn Abdullah, on the other hand, listened intently, then sighed and gave a wan little smile.

'And so I must return here for treatment until you are satisfied you were successful, and this treatment will take four years.'

Harry nodded, already apprised of His Excellency's views.

The Premier's black eyes brightened slyly, as though he'd put one over on Fate. 'You may be assured I'll be back every year, Doctor, and in the event I get perhaps another four years after that, I want to tell you something: I will endow Memorial Hospital with a million pounds.'

Harry smiled. 'Just get well,' he said, rising to his feet. 'That will be plenty of endowment for us.'

He held the old Arab's hand a moment, felt the faint pressure, squeezed back, then excused himself and left the room with Saud Haroush on his heels. Out in the corridor he said, 'Dr. Haroush; he's the most remarkable man I've met in many years. He's as strong as a giant.'

Haroush put his head to one side in the position of someone listening, and said, 'He is also very rich, Doctor, and when you get married you will find something among the presents to make you remember him.'

Harry, on the verge of walking away, gazed at the smaller man. 'Am I going to be married?' he asked.

Haroush smiled. 'Of course.'

Haroush hadn't actually had to have been very clairvoyant to work that out; after all, he had seen Harry and Regina together, had been with them in fact when they were together.

Harry smiled, 'Of course,' he echoed, and left the Middle-Easterner looking after him.

When he reached the office Albert Branch was impatiently waiting. He had a rolled-up sheaf of papers in one hand. 'I was telephoning around to find you,' he said. 'Well, no matter, you're here.' He handed Harry the roll of papers. 'Go over those, Harry, and tell me your candid opinion. They are outlines of the lectures I'll be giving. I want them to be word-perfect.'

Harry said he'd do it and put the papers aside. He explained where he'd been and how surprised he'd been to find His Excellency so well along the road to recovery. Dr. Branch nodded and furrowed his brow, then said, 'It is remarkable. I think I'll go and have a talk with him too. There might be something there worth incorporating into the newspaper column.' He smiled raffishly. 'I've accepted that offer to write a syndicated column for laymen.'

After the Old Man had departed Harry wryly considered that sheaf of typewritten pages and shook his head. He was already teetering on the brink of being more administrator than surgeon. This would push him still further in that direction.

He rang Regina and asked if she'd like to go for a drive with him that afternoon. She didn't ask why, nor where, all she wanted to know was what time he'd be at the house for her. He glanced at his wrist and said, 'Immediately after lunch; perhaps one o'clock,' and rang off.

Emily came down from the Chief Consultant's office to knock deferentially and enter. Harry was stuffing the lecture-papers into his pocket when he called out for her to come in.

Emily's clear eyes and handsome figure went with her clear complexion. If she had much vanity it didn't extend to colouring her hair which was a very attractive shade of grey. She said, 'Doctor, I've just spoken to the Chief. He said he'd already told you he was retiring from surgery.'

Harry nodded. He thought he understood what seemed to be troubling her and decided to help her with it. 'It's the arthritis; you know, as time passes, the crippling effects will become more pronounced. He's going to need quite a bit of secretarial help, Emily.'

Her face brightened. 'I know. Doctor, I've been with him a very long time . . .'

Harry stepped round the desk and put a hand lightly upon the older woman's shoulder. 'I understand, Emily; stay with him. He needs you now more than he needs anyone.'

She smiled, her eyes turning misty. 'I intend

to,' she said, and left Harry standing alone as she departed.

He glanced again at his watch. He would have time for lunch in the restaurant, but decided against eating there on two counts; the first one was that by now the news of the Old Man's retirement would be spreading throughout Memorial like wildfire and everyone would try to buttonhole him for confirmation. Secondly he wanted to have a leisurely, intimate luncheon with his fiancée, and therefore walked briskly down the corridor towards the lift, intending to bypass the restaurant.

He managed to get out of the building without being stopped, got into his car and drove away from Memorial with a crush of other cars on all sides. Not until then did he notice what a lovely day it had turned out to be. It was even warm out—unusual for this time of year—and the sky was clear. There was still evidence of the recent rain; puddles here and there, the washed-clean air, dirty clouds far away hovering on the horizon, but in his private world the sun was shining as it had never shone before.

Regina was ready and waiting although he arrived a little early. She ran out to meet him at the kerb, ready to confess smilingly she'd been watching for him from the sitting-room windows.

As they started away she said, 'Is this to be a

surprise, love, or am I allowed to guess where we're going?'

They were driving due south. He smiled at her. 'Leeswold?'

'Right; that would have been my guess. I'm going to have to dig out my old psychology books and try to fathom the fascination that little old country village has for you.'

He reached with one hand, pulled her closer and kept his arm round her waist as he drove out of the city on the arrow-straight, broad carriageway. 'There is an even greater fascination that possesses me that you might have more fun digging into.'

She put her head upon his shoulder. Her fragrance arose to tantalise him. He had completely forgotten the bulging sheaf of rolled papers in his pocket until she looked down to see what was between them, then he explained.

She said, 'I know. He read one of them to me at breakfast. I didn't understand very much of it, but Harry, you should have seen his expression. He's found a new fascinating career as a writer.' She snuggled closer. 'You're wonderful.'

He didn't dispute the allegation. He'd prefer to have her believe that in any case, but his private notion was that he hadn't contributed all that much towards solving the problem of her uncle.

The countryside swept past on both sides as

they sped along. After a while he said, 'This is going to be the longest month of my life—this waiting until the fifteenth.'

She pressed still closer and said nothing. Everything in her world, as in his, was sunshine and beautiful, and love-tinted.

We hope you have enjoyed this Large Print book. Other Chivers Press or G.K. Hall & Co. Large Print books are available at your library or directly from the publishers.

For more information about current and forthcoming titles, please call or write, without obligation, to:

Chivers Press Limited
Windsor Bridge Road
Bath BA2 3AX
England
Tel. (01225) 335336

OR

G.K. Hall & Co.
P.O. Box 159
Thorndike, Maine 04986
USA
Tel. (800) 223-2336

All our Large Print titles are designed for easy reading, and all our books are made to last.